A MODERN EXECUTIVE NOVEL

THE CHANGE UP

Leadership Growth Journeys

ANNISSA DESHPANDE

Published by Loglab, LLC
Editing, design, and distribution by Bublish

ISBN: 978-1-64704-940-9 (paperback)
ISBN: 978-1-64704-941-6 (eBook)
ISBN: 978-1-64704-942-3 (audiobook)

In loving memory of
Vinod Mama, Shama Mami, Nayana Atya, and Jamie Star.

The song is ended but the melody lingers on . . .

—Irving Berlin

CHAPTER 1

WITH ONE HAND gripping his sandy-blond hair and the other his mobile phone, Jack Shorn closed his eyes. "You talked to Shauna after the Johnston deal fell through? Okay, leave it with me, Brett. She'll be in my office in a few minutes."

"Shit!" he said as he hung up. *How the hell did we lose the Johnston deal? It was in the bag!* He'd just talked to the CEO last week, who'd been super gung ho. What happened?

Jack flung the phone on his desk and stretched back in his Herman Miller office chair to try to relieve the tension in his neck. Then he swerved to stare out his thirty-seventh-floor window, catching a glimpse of his exhausted expression against the backdrop of Atlanta's gloomy skyline. The warm spring rain that had been drenching the city for hours this Monday morning was finally tapering off, leaving behind dark, low clouds scattered among the skyscrapers.

It was hard to believe he'd been CEO of Accelx Services for fifteen months already. He'd been ecstatic to get the promotion and the opportunity to lead the workforce of three thousand employees. Driving sales as the company's Chief Revenue Officer for five years beforehand had positioned him well to help the company navigate its next phase of growth. And he felt very aligned with the company's mission—providing outsourced accounting services using its proprietary technology to save hospitals and long-term care facilities significant money each year. Gold Private Equity had bought the company fifteen months ago, recognizing significant growth opportunities in new verticals such as pharmaceuticals and medical devices. Despite all this, he still felt ill-equipped to handle the relentless challenges the role presented. He continued to gaze out the window, trying to chart the best way forward.

"Hey Jack." Shauna Miller-Desai, Accelx's Chief People Officer, knocked lightly on Jack's open door. "Do you need a minute?"

Jack spun around. "Hi. No, no, please come on in."

Shauna closed the door and walked across Jack's spacious corner office to take a seat at the maple conference table in the corner. "Everything okay?" she asked, removing a tablet from her satchel.

"Yeah. Just a challenging morning. We'll get through it." Jack made his way over and sat at the opposite end of the table. "But let's start with you. How are things going for you and the family? Everyone settling into the new house?"

"Yeah. It's nice to finally have a house close to my in-laws, and it's much bigger than what we had in Chicago." She smiled. "I can't believe it took over a year for us to find the place—tight market. Well, and we got distracted taking care of Ravi's dad."

"How's Sunil doing?" Jack asked after her father-in-law.

"Okay, I guess. He officially resigned from his CEO post last week. Said it wasn't fair to the company if he couldn't give his all." Shauna shook her head, fighting back tears. "Really hard decision for him. I'm so glad we're close by. His chemo is super draining. Ravi's over there every night."

"That's so tough. He led Elastitech impeccably for so many years. It's a big loss."

At that, a hint of a smile lifted Shauna's mouth. "He did. And he did so in such a humble way, always attributing their growth to his team and even a bit of luck." She looked at her tablet. "Anyway, thanks for asking. Shall we get to it?"

Jack looked down and brushed imaginary dust from the conference room table. "Before we get into your agenda, I want to talk to you about Brett."

"Oh?" Shauna straightened in her chair.

"Well, I know he talked to you about letting go of a few sales reps, but you were against it, so he backed off. I just wanted you to take another look. Now, more than ever, we need the right people. And frankly, as Chief Revenue Officer, Brett knows his current reps aren't a good fit."

Shauna leaned forward. "And Brett raised this with *you*?"

"Yes, just a few minutes ago," Jack replied. "I told him I'd talk to you."

"Hmm." Shauna sat back and straightened her shoulders. "I'm surprised. When we talked yesterday, Brett agreed we were *not* in a position to let these reps go. He gave each of them a good review and admitted he'd never provided any constructive performance feedback." She shook her head. "They all met the sales quota he'd established, so I guess I'm having a really hard time understanding how he's making the case that these sales reps aren't performing—and why he escalated this to you after our conversation."

"Shauna, they haven't made *any* inroads on strategic accounts."

"I understand, but we talked about this when we reviewed the sales incentive plan last year." Shauna laid both hands flat on the table. "You guys thought my suggestions were too aggressive, remember? Brett was worried it would disengage the sales team. We discussed the risk of this very thing happening, and Brett assured us he would manage the team to close strategic accounts."

Jack rubbed his forehead. "Look, everyone knew we needed to acquire at least *some* strategic accounts. That's all we've been talking about since I took this role. It's the whole thesis of

Gold's acquisition of Accelx. It's inexcusable for the sales reps not to deliver a single one!"

"Let's make sure we're focused on solving the *right* problem," Shauna retorted. "It's great to talk about the need for strategic accounts, but how is Brett setting his reps up for success? Has he trained them to penetrate these new markets?"

"Brett's spent a lot of time with his team," Jack said defensively. "He's been hands-on since he started in the role—just like he told us he would be!"

"Okay, but with all due respect," Shauna said, leaning in and lowering her voice, "does Brett know how to penetrate these new markets?"

"Of course he does!" Jack shook his head, as if trying to shake off an insult. "He's a seasoned sales leader. I've worked with the guy for years. He's the real deal."

Shauna took a slow, deep breath.

"Jack, do you remember that story I told you about the ops supervisor at my last company? You know, the one who was doing so well that we promoted him to the head of manufacturing, but he failed miserably in the new role?"

"Yeah, you said you ended up firing him after a short period of time, right?"

Shauna nodded. "That's the one. After six months, it was clear he wasn't a good fit—despite his past success. As much as we loved him and wanted him to thrive, we had to face the fact that his skills just didn't transfer to the bigger role."

"I know what you're getting at, but that's not the case with Brett. He can do this."

"Look, I know you have a soft spot for him, but the reality is he's struggling. The only strategic accounts we've landed this year have been the three *you* brought in. Brett certainly hasn't stepped up and closed one to show his team what the process looks like."

Jack shot up in his chair. "I don't have a soft spot for Brett. I just want to give him some time to find his legs in the new role. This is hard stuff. Even I had a hard time closing those accounts!"

"I get that, but we've also got to deal with investor expectations." Shauna sighed. "I'm merely suggesting that Brett may need some professional coaching to be able to operate at this new level."

"Well, he can't be successful without the right team around him," Jack snapped. "I'm just asking you to take another look."

"I can, but the bottom line is the reps did exactly what we incentivized them to do. They met quotas based on overall sales. We can't fire people for that." Shauna looked Jack in the eyes. "And, honestly, I'm a little surprised you're backing him up on this."

Jack studied Shauna's expression. She'd been working with him for about a year now, after a successful twelve-month stint as Chief People Officer at Dominal Industries in Chicago, another one of Gold's portfolio companies. Gold had recommended her to Jack for the Accelx role in Atlanta. They'd had a good initial rapport and still got along well personally. But as the company hit performance challenges in recent months, he'd started to feel tension between them.

"Look, you hired me to run the people dimension of this business." Shauna spoke slowly, choosing her words carefully. "We both respect Accelx's values, and we've talked about the importance of holding each other accountable to those values. It's the glue of any healthy culture. I've reviewed this situation from multiple angles, and I just can't justify letting good reps go when my concerns are more about their leader."

Jack glanced at his smartwatch as a notification came in. "We'll have to finish this discussion later. I know it's important. But the board just scheduled an impromptu call, and I need to prepare. Do you have anything urgent on your list?"

"Nothing that can't wait." Shauna placed her tablet back in her satchel. "Listen, I'm more than willing to reconsider—if there's something I'm missing. But I just don't believe we are focused on the right issues."

"Thanks, Shauna," Jack said, meaning it. "You know I always appreciate your perspective—even when it doesn't align with mine. Let's reconnect tomorrow after I've had a chance to talk to the board and Brett some more."

"Sure." She waved as she walked out the door. "Good luck with the board call."

CHAPTER 2

AFTER SHAUNA LEFT his office, Jack sat back in his chair and closed his eyes, enjoying a rare moment to breathe. After a few minutes, he shook his head and stood up from his desk.

Scanning his empty office, Jack remembered how much he disliked the brushed nickel and maple modern décor his predecessor had selected. It felt so indistinct, like every other professional services office in the country. In his first few months as CEO, he had experimented with the artwork to try to personalize the space a bit—everything from thin, black-framed

Atlanta skyline photos to modernist paintings. While he'd settled on the modernist paintings, he still didn't feel like his office reflected who he was. It wasn't an environment that helped calm his nerves, which he needed more than ever these days. *Never mind,* he thought, *that's a challenge for another day. Concentrate! Look at the problems right in front of you.*

Jack closed his eyes and clasped his hands behind his head to cradle it. *The board . . .* He tried to focus for a few minutes, but his mind wandered.

Why can't I catch a break? When did this get so hard? Everyone constantly needed something from him—the board, his team, the employees, the customers. He felt like he was always playing whack-a-mole, but with a million fires to stomp out. *This isn't what I thought it'd be like.*

Jack opened his eyes, unclasped his hands, and straightened up.

What could this board meeting be about? he wondered. There was no new data. He knew they needed to start hitting their strategic account numbers, but they'd hit that message pretty hard already. *What am I missing?*

He walked around his desk to the other side of it, where he'd sat so many times before becoming CEO. This was where he'd explained all the sales numbers and revenue opportunities to his predecessor.

"It can't be Brett," he said aloud, staring across the imposing desk as if still answering to a CEO. *He's helped me hit the numbers all these years. He knows the players and the industry.*

He's the one who helped me understand this place when I was just starting out.

Jack replayed the last conversation he'd had with his predecessor, Chris Meis, before assuming the role of CEO. Chris had been wary of Brett becoming the CRO. What was it Chris said? Brett wasn't proactive enough? What if Shauna was on to something? Why hadn't Brett given his reps any feedback? In the past, he would have come to Jack to discuss the feedback he was going to give, making sure it resonated and hit the right points. *We haven't had a conversation like that in a while. I just assumed he was doing it all along. Maybe his back is against the wall and he's feeling it. I've got to keep supporting him.*

Jack brought the fingertips of both hands together in front of his chest and tapped gently.

I've got to make more time, dig deep. Maybe we should review the latest outreach metrics together. Wait . . . have I seen those lately?

He sat up in his chair, opened his email, and scrolled for a message from Brett. *That's weird, no outreach metrics since January.* He shot off an email request and leaned back in his chair.

He needed to help Brett figure out his team—and get Shauna onboard too. Maybe the three of them should talk. But did he really want Shauna there? Brett could be so stubborn. *Screw it! We'll all meet. Maybe it will help Shauna understand Brett's perspective better.*

His thoughts wandered back to the upcoming board meeting. Maybe the board wanted to talk about the Onergize implementation. He knew it had been bumpy, but he'd been pretty clear that their first strategic account might be. No, the team had been responsive, so that couldn't be it.

What if it was someone else on the team? They'd been all over him about Rob, but he was making progress. They wouldn't be ready to support Onergize without Rob's technical skills. *He might not always act like a CTO, but sometimes we've just gotta get shit done.* But Rob hasn't had any recent interactions with them, so he didn't think that was it either.

Don had met with a few board members yesterday—maybe he did something? *He's got such a know-it-all-attitude—typical CFO.* But Jack was sure Don would have said something to him if there was an issue. *Maybe he didn't pick up on it? Wouldn't be the first time.* But last time, Guillermo just called Jack directly. He wouldn't convene the entire board for something like that.

Can't be Shauna—she's earned their trust. He didn't think it was Hannah either, though the board did say she sometimes didn't show up like the COO. Also, he'd coached her on it, and the last board meeting seemed to go better. She was probably the least of their problems by now.

Jack shook his head, exhaled loudly, and tried to quiet his thoughts.

"Why the hell are we meeting?" he whispered out loud.

He caught a glimpse of the framed picture of his beaming family on the day he was promoted to CEO. He loved that picture and made sure it stayed in a prominent place on his desk.

Dang, Bridget was so proud, he thought, noticing a few rays of sunshine peeking through the dark, low clouds outside. Jack hoped it was a sign that the surprise board meeting would go smoothly. *I've never failed before, and I'm certainly not going to start now!*

He checked his watch and saw it was 10:30 a.m. He went back around his desk, sitting again in his chair. Jack straightened his shoulders and took a deep breath as he clicked on the video call link to join the board meeting. As he waited to connect, he sat perfectly still, his hands folded on his desk. After what felt like an eternity, the screen flashed and revealed the six board members of Accelx seated around a long, U-shaped oak conference table. Behind them, Jack could make out the New York skyline.

"Jack." Tom Johansen, managing partner at Gold Private Equity, smiled as Jack's video and audio connected. "Thanks for making the time on such short notice."

Jack was relieved to see Tom, who was an old friend from his MBA days. Over the years, Tom had been supportive and looked for opportunities to bring Jack into the Gold portfolio. He'd been especially excited when Gold acquired Accelx. Jack knew Tom couldn't help him much in this meeting, even as a board member, but it was still comforting to see a friendly face.

"Hi everyone." Jack gave a wave to the screen with his right hand and started pumping a soccer stress ball off camera with his left hand. "Nice to see you all."

"I'm sure you're wondering why we've called this meeting, Jack," Guillermo Jose, Gold's CEO, said as he smoothed his maroon V-neck sweater. "Yesterday, I was at a charity fund-raiser here in New York and ran into the CEO of Onergize, one of your new strategic accounts."

Jack nodded. "Onergize is our first strategic account implementation."

"Yes, Bernard mentioned that," Guillermo continued. "He said you told him to expect it to be a bit bumpy but that your team would stay on top of things and respond immediately."

"That's right. I wanted to be as transparent as possible, and my team has been making sure we quickly resolve issues as they arise."

"The problem is that Bernard said his team is quite frustrated with the implementation. He complained about not getting the proper support from Accelx and told me he's questioning whether he made the right decision."

"Ah." Jack took a deep breath. "I am aware that there are some implementation issues, but the team is all over it. I'm surprised to hear they don't feel like they're getting the right support. They have the direct involvement of our COO and CTO on a daily basis."

Guillermo cleared his throat. "Be that as it may, your team isn't making your new client feel as though they have things under control. So, unfortunately, the first strategic account you've closed is now at risk."

"I appreciate the heads-up." Jack said, trying to sound confident. "I will go back to the team right after this call and personally get involved to resolve any outstanding issues."

"Okay. But Jack, how many things are you going to get personally involved in?" Guillermo seemed to stare right into Jack's eyes. "The three strategic accounts you've brought in so far have been due to your personal efforts. There's no question you're talented, but you're the CEO now. Your job isn't to do everything yourself; it's to get your team to execute to achieve these goals."

"I understand. Believe me, I don't want to be doing everything either, I'm working to get the team operating more effectively."

Jack felt increasingly small as he watched the board members exchange glances amid an uncomfortable silence. He was starting to sweat, and he hoped nothing was visible over video.

"Jack," Renata Campbell, another managing partner, chimed in, "you know we had concerns about the leadership team when you took the role of CEO. That's why we asked you to take a hard look. Your predecessor was a good CEO for a single-vertical company, but we didn't think he could lead Accelx to the next level. We were frank with you about the fact that the leadership team wasn't operating at the right level. I mean, your CTO was elevated to the role based on his technical genius, but we're concerned about his leadership skills. He continues to do the bulk of the work instead of leading his team."

"I'm working on that with him, but honestly, our backs have been against the wall. There's no way we could have been ready to support big, strategic accounts from a technology perspective without his efforts this past year," Jack defended. "I admit there are still glitches we need to work through, but given everything at stake here, I've got to be thoughtful about how I make changes to the team. There's a lot of institutional knowledge there."

The room fell silent again and all eyes shifted to Guillermo, who was clearly listening but staring out a corner window, deep in thought. Only his commanding side profile was visible to Jack, whose chest tightened as he waited for Guillermo to speak. It felt like a courtroom scene where the judge was about to read the verdict. After a few endless moments, Guillermo turned to face the camera.

"Jack, I know you're working hard to make things happen at Accelx." Guillermo spoke slowly, enunciating each word. "But it's not enough. You know our investment thesis. We didn't buy Accelx for the status quo. The growth we need to see for a proper return on our investment means you must penetrate new verticals and effectively service those new accounts. This means you have to shift your team's focus, retool, and reorganize to support a broader set of customers."

"Understood, sir." Jack started to bite his lower lip but forced himself to stop.

"Do you?" Guillermo leaned forward. "Because we've had similar conversations about your team a few times now and nothing seems to have changed. I understand and even respect your loyalty to people you've worked with for a long time, but something isn't right here. Something isn't clicking. Things need to change now."

Jack nodded as he pumped the stress ball furiously below his desk.

"In case I am not being clear," Guillermo said, leaning slightly forward, "consider this your final warning. You're getting a mandate. You have ninety days to show significant progress on strategic accounts and get within twenty-five percent of the revenue target in that sector. And this can't just be you bringing in and nurturing new business; your team must do their part to close new deals and keep these new strategic customers happy. Also, I expect your team to turn Onergize around *fast*. Don't lose this account," he stressed. "If you and your team don't meet this mandate in ninety days, we will be having a very different conversation about your future at Accelx. Have I made myself clear?"

Jack's green eyes widened. "Crystal clear, sir. I won't let you down." Forget the courtroom, now Jack felt like a kid in the principal's office.

"Good." Guillermo picked up his tablet and stood. "I think we're done here." The CEO of Gold began walking out of the room, and Jack continued to sit respectfully.

"And Jack?" Guillermo stopped and turned back to look directly at him with a softer expression. "I know what you're doing is challenging. Making these transitions to the leadership team means looking deep at yourself, your relationship with your team, and their relationship with one another. We don't know what's stalling the growth, but you must figure this out. We want you to succeed—and we believe you can. Let us know how we can help."

"Of course, Guillermo, thank you." Jack watched Guillermo make his way out of the room, along with several other board members. Guillermo was at least a head taller than the rest of them. Tom stood and gave a quick, encouraging thumbs-up to Jack before picking up his coffee cup and heading toward the door.

"Jack, could you stay on a moment?" Renata asked.

Before Jack could answer, Tom's head popped back on screen.

"Hey, bud." Tom took a few steps back so he could get a better look at Jack. "Hang in there, okay? You've got this. I'll check in with you later."

"Thanks." Jack smiled halfheartedly.

Tom waved and made his way out of the conference room. Renata moved to a chair in the center of the room, closer to the camera.

"Look," Renata said, clearing her throat, "I know we've talked about this a few times, but I really think you need an executive coach to help you through this. Guillermo's not messing around. You're on a short leash now."

Jack slumped visibly. "I know, but I don't think an executive coach is the answer. If I could just—"

"Jack." Renata cut him off. "We were very clear when we gave you this role that we had concerns about your leadership team—yet you've taken no action."

Jack put both of his hands flat on his desk. "Renata, that's not fair. I've been working with each member of my executive team on the areas we all identified. They're making progress."

"Sorry, but it's too little, too late." Renata pushed a stray strand of brown hair away from her face. "We're just not seeing it. Look, I've been down this road before with CEOs. Even if you have the right executive team—which I'm not sure you do—they're not working together to achieve important strategic goals. Frankly, I'm not sure you're even focused on the right things."

Jack rubbed his forehead. "I'm focused on sales and implementation. Isn't that all that matters?"

"Well, not exactly," Renata replied. "You're building a totally new way of selling and servicing to an industry your team hasn't handled before. While you may have some experience to build upon from your days as Chief Revenue Officer, you're now the CEO. It's totally different."

"Yes," Jack agreed, "which is why I don't have time to meet with a coach right now. I need to focus on building this new way of selling and making sure these next few implementations go well. I'm sure you can understand my time constraints."

Jack watched Renata inhale deeply. He could practically feel her frustration through the screen.

"I had a feeling you'd be reluctant, so I took the liberty of setting up a meeting with a coach I know well. She has helped a number of CEOs and executive leaders across the Gold portfolio."

"I see. So, you're not really giving me a choice."

"Meg's available for a call tomorrow at three p.m. Eastern. And here's a final piece of advice." Renata leaned forward. "Keep an open mind. Whether you realize it or not, this is the best thing for you, for your leadership team, for Accelx, and for Gold."

CHAPTER 3

"HI DADDY!" JACK'S four-year-old son, Jamie, waved from the backyard at his father's second-story home office window before propelling himself down the slide of their play set. The late afternoon sun lit up the backyard with an iridescent glow.

Jack smiled and gave Jamie a thumbs-up. He cherished the days when he was able to pick up his kids from daycare and finish his workday at home, even if it made for later nights in order to get everything done.

"Daddy! Me next. Watch!" His two-year old daughter, Quinn, scrambled to the top of the slide, with the kids' nanny in tow.

Jack stood long enough to watch Quinn make it to the bottom, tumble into the lush grass, and clap in delight. He blew her a kiss before making his way back to the traditional cherrywood desk in his cozy wood-paneled office. It was a few minutes before 3:00 p.m., and he had one last call to make before dinner and bath time with the kids.

He settled into his emerald leather office chair and took a long sip from the water bottle on his desk. "Video time," he said out loud, his voice heavy.

"Hi Jack, glad you could make it," Renata greeted him. "Looks like you had pickup duty today?"

"Hi Renata," Jack replied. "Yes. Today, I'm on duty. The kids are outside playing with the nanny, so we shouldn't have any interruptions."

"Good." Renata seemed to catch herself and smiled. "I mean, not that we mind interruptions from the kids. We're all doing our best here. I want to introduce you to Meg Beecham, the executive coach I mentioned."

"Hi Jack. It's great to meet you." Meg smiled.

Jack studied the woman in the bottom window of his screen. She had a mix of white and blonde hair, neatly styled in a bob cropped about two inches above her shoulders. If he had to wager, he'd guess she was in her mid-fifties. She was wearing a white blouse with faint silver pinstripes and had the sleeves rolled up to her elbows like she was ready to get down to business.

"Hi Meg. It's good to meet you too. Thanks for making the time."

"So, Jack," Renata started, "Meg has thirty years of experience in HR, IT, finance, and strategy, and has held a number of significant executive roles at Fortune 150 companies. She started her coaching practice about eight years ago. As I mentioned to you yesterday, many of our portfolio company leaders have been successfully coached by her."

"That's great to hear, Renata."

"Meg," Renata continued, "in addition to being a terrific hands-on dad, Jack is a first-time CEO of Accelx, which we invested in fifteen months ago. He's got a strong background in sales and revenue at Accelx and other companies. I sent you the background materials on the company, along with Gold's investment thesis, to give you an understanding of their business. Essentially, they've got a tall order right now to penetrate new markets, and I think Jack could benefit from your coaching."

"Understood." Meg smiled and straightened in her chair.

"Okay, I am going to leave you two to take it from here. Sound good?"

"Of course, Renata." Meg waved goodbye. "Thanks again."

"Yeah, thanks," Jack mumbled.

Meg looked a bit perplexed. "That was interesting."

"What?" Jack asked.

"Renata never joins introductory calls like that." Meg tilted her head. "Do you know why she joined this one?"

"Ha!" Jack laughed nervously. "I think she wanted to make sure I'd show up."

"Do you typically blow off calls?" Meg inquired with a hint of sarcasm.

"No, not really," Jack replied. "Actually, never. I just think this meeting is very important to her."

"To *her*? Why?"

Jack leaned back and rested his palms on the curved arms of his chair. He heard the faint echo of his kids chatting away on the swings in the backyard and was quiet for a moment while he considered Meg's question.

Finally, he said, "Honestly, I think she's worried about Accelx and Gold's investment—maybe even a little bit about me as the company's CEO."

Meg nodded slowly. "Are *you* worried?"

"No . . . Well, maybe a little. The board meeting yesterday was pretty tough. But I'm doing everything I can." Jack leaned forward and rubbed his eyes. "I get that the board is frustrated, but we're doing hard stuff, and it takes time. Did she give you any more background?" he asked, trying to read Meg's expression.

"She mentioned you provide outsourced accounting services to hospitals and long-term care facilities and are trying to break into some other adjacent verticals," Meg stated. "I'll review the materials she sent over to get a deeper understanding of what you do."

Jack nodded. "It's actually more than just outsourced accounting services. We have a proprietary technology that automates accounting and billing, making the process faster and more efficient. Our clients save millions. Did she say anything else?"

"Just that Accelx has been in the portfolio for a little over a year and that she thought you may need some coaching."

"Yeah, she said the same thing to me after yesterday's board meeting." Jack looked down. "It's not the first time she's mentioned it. I haven't been very open to the idea."

"Why not?"

"I'm already stretched thin." Jack sighed. "And not to be rude, but I'm not sure coaching will add value. I mean, do you even know anything about my business?"

"Do you know anything about mine?" Meg retorted, giving Jack the side-eye.

"Touché," Jack shot back, a hint of a smile on his face. "Tell me about how you help businesses."

"Actually, I help leaders, and this helps the businesses they run." Meg picked up a Slinky Junior from her desk and let her words sink in. "You see, when I'm asked to advise companies, most of the time I find they have a team of leaders, not a leadership team. Does that help clarify?"

"Interesting."

"Jack, do you think you have an aligned leadership team?"

"Yes, I do."

"Well, in my experience, most CEOs believe this, because they have good relationships with each of the leaders on their team." Meg let the Slinky move back and forth from hand to hand as she spoke. "But just because the CEO has a great relationship with everyone doesn't guarantee that everyone else gets along with one another. Most of the time they don't—even though they play nice in front of the boss. But behind the scenes, they're often advocating for their specific functions instead of working together toward the company's strategic goals."

Jack folded his hands in his lap. "Okay, but that's still pretty vague."

"I'm a coach. In general, you know what a coach does, right?"

"Of course!" Jack fidgeted with his folded hands. "I coach my kids' soccer teams. I get coaching, but I struggle to see how it helps in the business world. I know some other executives who work with coaches, but I'm not sure it's necessary in this case."

"Okay, noted," Meg replied. "But just like with sports, you have a team of people trying to get something done, and they need guidance."

"Hmm." Jack crossed his arms. "Isn't that the leader's job?"

"Yes, exactly. That *is* the leader's job." Meg put her Slinky down. "So, why do you think Renata is worried about you, Accelx, and Gold's investment?"

"The investors think we need to penetrate new verticals to achieve expected growth goals and expand the business. Unfortunately, in fifteen months, we've only acquired three strategic accounts, and that's been due to my efforts, not our sales team's efforts." Jack sighed. "Now, one of the strategic accounts we acquired is unsatisfied. I get it, the board is frustrated, and they think we're not operating effectively."

"How many strategic accounts did you commit to closing by this date?" Meg asked.

"We committed to hit an overall revenue goal, with thirty percent of it coming from strategic accounts," Jack told her. "We've met the revenue numbers, just not in the right verticals. I'm disappointed in our progress. But with my sales background, I know it takes time to penetrate new verticals."

"What expectation did you set with your team in terms of strategic accounts?"

"They know that Gold's entire growth thesis hinges on acquiring strategic accounts." Jack leaned forward. "These are seasoned leaders; they know what to do."

"And yet they haven't delivered."

"Like I said, it's just going to take time," Jack replied, trying not to get defensive. "We are all working hard to achieve the goal."

Meg leaned back in her chair and seemed to be deep in thought. Jack could hear Jamie and Quinn kicking the soccer ball into the goal he had set up in the backyard last month. How he wished he could be with them rather than on this call.

"Your silence is scaring me," Jack said after a few moments. "What are you thinking?"

"Sorry." Meg snapped back to attention. "Just gathering my thoughts. I assume you like sports since you coach soccer, let me ask you something."

"Sure, love sports, particularly soccer."

"Okay, no matter the sport, the goal is pretty straightforward, right? Win the game."

"Of course."

"And, for arguments sake, let's say the talent on *your* team is the best in the world, okay?"

Jack nodded.

"Yet, every team has different personalities that require different coaching techniques, strategies, and tactics to beat the competition, right?"

"Yeah," Jack agreed. "But that's sports, not business."

"It's no different," Meg countered. "Based on what you've shared so far, it sounds like it's possible you might be *assuming* everyone is aligned on the plays—but what if they're not?"

Jack leaned back in his chair. "I'm not sure I follow."

Meg picked up her Slinky again. "The number one issue I see with leadership teams is misalignment among members. I'm more of a baseball fan than a soccer fan, so imagine if the pitcher was only focused on his part of the game and declared victory if his pitching was perfect regardless of whether the team won or not. That doesn't make sense, right?"

"Of course not, but I don't think that's our issue."

"Well, give it some thought. It's just one idea—all part of the brainstorming process to see what's causing your challenges."

Jack glanced at his smartwatch. "I appreciate your time, Meg. Unfortunately, I have some things I need to get done before the end of the day. I know it's important to Renata that we work together, so what's the next step?"

"To be honest, you need to think hard about whether *you* want to work with me." Meg put her Slinky down on her desk again. "I only take on clients who are willing to put in the necessary time and effort to drive real change."

"I understand. It's just that work is super challenging right now." Jack sighed. "I don't know where to find another minute in my day."

"We can work on that too. But you're only going to see results if you fully commit to the process."

"I get it. Give me a few days to think everything over," Jack replied.

"Sure. Let's regroup next week. Sound good?"

"Okay, thanks, Meg. I don't mean to be short. It really was great meeting you," he said, waving at the camera.

Jack disconnected from the meeting and laid his head against the back of his chair, his hands covering his face. He listened for the kids outside but heard nothing. He exhaled loudly, feeling like he'd just lost precious minutes of his overpacked life to a conversation that didn't get him any closer to making progress toward his goals.

CHAPTER 4

**MARCH 17
3:08 P.M.**

"THANKS AGAIN FOR meeting me here." Shauna placed a tray with a pitcher of iced tea, two glasses filled to the brim with ice, and a plate of freshly baked chocolate chip cookies on the wicker table. She managed a tired smile and then took a seat across from Jack.

The air was thick, tempered by an occasional breeze permeating the screened patio and gently shaking the leaves of the oak and magnolia trees framing the expansive yard. Although grateful for the fresh air, Jack had to roll up the sleeves of his blue checkered shirt to get some relief from the humidity.

"No problem. It's probably better that we have this meeting out of the office." Jack watched several lovebugs scurry across the patio screen. "I'm excited I got to see your new house, though I wish it were under better circumstances. How's Sunil doing?"

"Not great." Shauna poured iced tea into each of the glasses. "He's sleeping now. Because it's a single story, our house is so much easier for him to navigate after chemo."

"Makes sense." Jack took a sip of iced tea. "When will Ravi be back?"

"Tonight. It was just an overnight trip for work." Shauna rubbed her eyes. "I'm sorry, I haven't been sleeping too well."

Jack's brow furrowed out of concern. "You know we're all here for you guys, whatever you need."

"Thanks, I know. We've been fortunate to have a lot of great support. Did I tell you the old Dominal crew has been finding reasons to come down to Atlanta?" Shauna chuckled. "Jen, my old boss, was here last week under the guise of an important meeting with a candidate she was supposedly recruiting. Michelle, the CEO, said there was a potential acquisition in Atlanta and came up last month. And Mark, our old CEO, is coming in two weeks for a conference. It's all very sweet."

Jack smiled warmly. "That's really nice. I'm glad you've stayed close to them and they're being so supportive. Are your folks still planning to come out next month?"

"Well, since Sunil has been struggling so much, we've asked them to be on deck to come out for a prolonged period of time." Shauna bit her lower lip, trying to hold back tears. "You know . . . if things don't get better. Over the years, when Ravi and I were dating and then engaged, they spent a lot of time with Sunil and Shilpa. It's nice. The in-laws are close friends. Not every couple gets that. I'm grateful. And of course, they want to be here for Ravi and me."

"Well, you've definitely got the space," Jack commented. "It's a beautiful home. I love the ranch style."

"Thanks." Shauna took out her tablet. "Should we get to business?"

"Yeah." Jack lifted his iced tea to eye level. "I may need something stronger after reading your executive summary and reviewing the report you sent."

Shauna laughed. "Don't worry, we have plenty of whiskey. Just say when."

"Deal!" Jack smiled and put his glass down on the coaster. Then he reached into his bag, pulled out his tablet, and clicked on the employee engagement report Shauna had sent him. He studied the graphs for a moment. "Well, you warned me to expect a dip in engagement given the organizational change we're experiencing. It's disappointing but not surprising—though the dip is bigger than I expected. What other things should I be thinking about?"

Shauna sat back in her chair and studied her tablet, using her finger to scroll up and down through the report for a few moments. "Yes, at this point, I'd like it to be higher, but given our slow progress on strategic accounts, it makes sense. What's more concerning to me is the feedback on the leadership team starting on page four."

Jack scrolled down and started to read through the comments. He could feel his breathing quicken as the words screamed at him from the page. *No collaboration. Bureaucracy. Competing priorities. Micromanagement.* He put his tablet on the table and took in the sound of the birds chirping in the yard. Finally, he leaned forward to grab a chocolate chip cookie from the tray.

"These comments drive me to stress eat." Jack took a bite of the warm cookie. "Wow! These are fantastic! Homemade?"

"My mother-in-law stress bakes." Shauna grabbed a cookie and smiled. "Jack, I'm going to develop a plan to start addressing these problem areas with specific actions, but I'm going to need your help. I can't do this alone."

"Engagement is your number one priority, right?" Jack finished off his cookie and grabbed another as Shauna nodded. "I get it, but just to be straightforward with you, I do have other things I have to get done first, particularly with what I told you happened during the board meeting earlier this week."

"Understood. But these engagement problems all point to the leadership team's behavioral issues." Shauna took a long sip of iced tea. "Addressing the lack of collaboration and competing priorities is key for us to meet the board's ninety-day mandate. If we want to get things back on track quickly, we'll need to be aligned to coach each leader on these topics."

Jack washed down his cookie with iced tea and brushed the crumbs off his hand. He picked up his tablet again to re-read page four. Shaking his head, he said, "Okay, I'm listening. What do you have in mind?"

"Hannah and Don," Shauna began. "Both of their teams had the lowest ratings on collaboration."

"Is the low rating really about collaboration, or do they not want friction?" Jack asked. "Healthy friction is good between finance and other departments. I want Don's team asking tough questions and making sure we're using our resources properly."

"I agree finance should ask tough questions. But Don's team takes this to another level. They create roadblocks to getting anything done."

"We have to be careful because we're not meeting our investor objectives right now," Jack pointed out. "Making sure we're managing our finances carefully is crucial. We don't want to give the board another thing to hold against us."

Shauna nodded. "Right, but we still have to make strategic investments to be successful. We can't be penny-wise and pound-foolish. The other day, during a meeting I was in, Don and Hannah went at it about resources. Hannah had a budget she needed approved to support Onergize's implementation, and Don flat out said no. Neither of them shared any perspective or debated. They just talked at each other."

Jack sighed. "Without any context, I can't say if that's wrong or right."

"Who's right or wrong isn't the problem. The issue is they're not communicating well, and they are constantly at each other's throats. It's impacting team morale and pulling people in different directions when everyone needs to be working together to achieve important strategic goals. We've got to address this to be able to meet our ninety-day mandate. Does that make sense?"

"Yes, it does," Jack reluctantly agreed. "What else?"

"Then there's Rob," Shauna continued. "His team feels underutilized and micromanaged. We know he has a tendency to do the work and not lead his team to get the work done. We have to fix this."

"C'mon." Jack set his tablet back on the table. "You know we were under the gun to get our software ready for strategic accounts. Rob said it was the only way."

"And you believed him? It seems to me that this is his MO for *every* situation," Shauna argued. "We have some top-tier tech talent on that team. My understanding is that many came for the opportunity to work with Rob. Now, they're saying it feels like they are watching Rob work. They're all going to walk out the door soon if we don't fix this."

"You know I hate it when you throw the 'talent will walk out the door' statement at me," Jack said. "If people don't want to be at Accelx, let them leave."

"Listen, we both agree we don't want to keep people who aren't aligned to our values. But if talent is leaving because their skills aren't being utilized, that's a very different problem," Shauna said, shaking her head. "If you want Rob to do all the coding, then he shouldn't be our CTO. You know he's way too expensive to just be a coder."

Jack refilled his glass with iced tea and then slumped back in his chair, trying to release the mounting tension in his shoulders. He surveyed the entire backyard and inhaled the scent of freshly manicured grass. He tried to focus on the sound of trickling water coming from the ceramic fountain that had been strategically positioned in the middle of the lawn. He was exhausted and searching for the energy he needed to finish this difficult conversation. He closed his eyes briefly and took a slow, calming breath.

"You know I've been working on this problem with Rob," Jack said quietly. "I know it's a scarce commodity right now, but we have to give him time."

"He's had time. Things haven't changed. You told me that the board even called the problem out earlier this week," Shauna stated emphatically. "We need a different approach. I understand you're busy. Let me take the lead on this and we can discuss. That's all I'm suggesting right now. Okay?"

"Okay." Jack said slowly. "What else? Brett?"

Shauna nodded. "Yeah. Unfortunately, his team lacks confidence in his leadership. Plus, he doesn't seem to listen and lacks self-awareness. Several people on his team noted that he's always pushing his own agenda. Just take a look at some of these comments."

"Ouch! That's bad." Jack picked up his tablet and read through the comments. "*Oi*, really bad. This is a complex problem, though. We've got to dig a bit deeper to understand what's happening here. Some of it may be the team too. Let's stick with our plan to work through the feedback and see where we end up."

"Okay." Shauna smiled tentatively and scrolled through more of the report.

"So, I guess that leaves me?" Jack ran his fingers through his hair.

Shauna nodded and refilled her iced tea glass, then very slowly squeezed a few drops from a bright-yellow lemon wedge. She appeared to be stalling as she took a long, drawn-out sip.

Jack grinned. "Do you need something stronger in that tea before we have this conversation?"

Shauna shook her head and swallowed. "No, no, really, it's not that bad."

Jack leaned forward. "Okay, lay it on me. I can handle it."

"Well, sixty percent of the company has confidence in you as the CEO. Sure, we'd like that to be higher, but it's still the majority and not bad given our current performance and the fact that you're a first-time CEO." Shauna took a deep breath. "But the company doesn't see you holding your team accountable, and they feel like you don't communicate enough. This came out in the ratings as well as the comments."

"Interesting." Jack crossed his arms and leaned back in his chair. He sat in silence for a few moments, processing this information. "Sorry, but that makes no sense, I feel like I'm *always* communicating. I have monthly all-hands calls and quarterly emails. I even have an open-door policy for anyone to come talk to me."

"Yeah, but I'm not sure those messages are landing the right way." Shauna took another sip of her iced tea.

"What do you mean?" Jack felt a headache coming on.

Shauna handed the plate of cookies to Jack, and he reluctantly took another, ashamed of his lack of willpower.

"Do you remember when I told you I worked with a coach at Dominal?"

"Yeah," Jack nodded. "Meg. I met with her yesterday."

"What?" Shauna seemed surprised. "I didn't know you were looking for a coach."

"I'm not," Jack said, shaking his head. "At least, I don't think I am. But Renata insisted we meet."

"Ah." Shauna nodded. "Meg's great! She met Sunil at my wedding and ended up doing some work with him and his team at Elastitech over the past few years. Sunil was impressed. They had great outcomes."

"That's good to hear." Jack took a bite of his cookie.

"Just so you know, I haven't spoken to her about anything work related since I left Dominal," Shauna clarified. "But the best thing she taught me and my former boss, Jen, was that all our communications had to emphasize what was in it for the audience."

Jack swallowed the last bite of his cookie and vowed not to take another. "I don't follow."

"Well, I've been thinking that maybe we're communicating what we think people need to know instead of what they want to know in order to be able to take action," Shauna explained. "Even I still fall into the trap of failing to consider my audience's perspective. That's when I have to stop and readjust in order to adapt to their frame of reference—you know, to fine-tune my message for *them*."

"That actually makes a lot of sense," Jack said, nodding. "We do this in sales all the time. We need messaging that resonates with our customer. It's the same principle, right?"

"Yep! See, you already have the skillset, you just need to apply it to the workforce now."

Jack smiled and sat quietly, taking everything in, including the sparrows chirping noisily in the yard like they were trading the latest bird gossip. He hoped their chatter could silence the negativity swirling around his brain. *Can I do anything right?*

"Would you like to hear some of the comments?" Shauna said, breaking the silence. "Sunil always says that's where you find the gold nuggets to drive real change."

Jack looked at her and took a deep breath. He wasn't sure he could take much more.

"He's right," he whispered. Then he said more loudly, "But maybe later. You've given me a lot to digest, and I want to dig into it all. Could send me a summary of the comments tomorrow?"

"Of course!" Shauna made a note in her tablet. "How about that whiskey now? You look like you could use one."

Jack forced a smile. "Shauna, I would love nothing more than to sit here in your beautiful backyard and share a whiskey with you. But I think we both have important things to take care of right now." He nodded toward the house.

Shauna sighed. "You're right, but I wish you weren't. Rain check?"

"Absolutely." Jack placed his tablet in his bag and stood up. "Look, I know this was a hard conversation for you to have with me, but I appreciate your directness. Thanks for keeping me honest. I look forward to seeing your approach on these issues."

"Ah, this"—Shauna wagged her finger back and forth in the space between the two of them—"is healthy friction. We didn't talk *at* each other but talked *to* each other, discussing, debating, working to understand each other's perspectives, and developing a plan to move forward that works for both of us."

"Agreed!" Jack exclaimed. "This is how I want to get our team operating."

Shauna smiled. "Thanks again for coming over. I'll be back in the office tomorrow for the team meeting."

"Brace yourself," Jack laughed as they both stood up and made their way into the house and toward the front door. "I have a feeling it's going to be an interesting day."

CHAPTER 5

THE FOLLOWING MORNING, Jack turned the corner just outside his office and headed to the breakroom to fill his coffee mug before the leadership team meeting. It was Thursday, the only day he asked everyone come in. As a result, it had become the logical day for the weekly meeting. While he'd had individual conversations about the board's message over the past three days, this was the first time everyone would be together for a discussion. Walking past all the photos of Accelx's employees living the company's values, he noticed the "Do What You Say;

Say What You Do!" poster just outside Brett's office. He came to a sudden stop when he distinctly heard Shauna's raised voice coming from inside.

"Brett, what the hell are you playing at? Jack's wondering why I'm not supporting your recommendation to terminate your reps. But you agreed the other day they did *exactly* what you asked them to do. And you didn't give them any performance feedback, so you don't have grounds to terminate them."

"Well . . . yeah . . ." Jack heard Brett stammer, ". . . uh, sorry, Shauna. My back's against the wall. The reps just aren't getting it done. We're in a tough spot. I don't have time to performance manage these guys. We just need to pay them out and move on."

"No way!" Shauna snapped.

Wow, Jack thought. *She's really upset.*

"You shouldn't have gone behind my back. We should be escalating issues to Jack together, when needed. And besides, it's your job to give your reps feedback and help them meet their goals. I get you're feeling pressure, but you're the one who needs to lead this team to success. We could've brainstormed about how to turn things around. But you went to Jack and made it seem like I was doing something wrong—like I wasn't willing to work with you. I mean, what the hell?"

"Okay, okay, I get it. I . . ." Jack thought Brett sounded tongue-tied but apologetic. "I agree. It was a crappy way to handle it. I guess I just panicked."

"Yeah, by throwing your reps and me under the bus?" Shauna reminded him.

"I didn't mean to. I'm sorry. Maybe we could brainstorm together later today."

"Yeah, okay." Shauna said. "Just let me know. Hey, we better go. The team meeting starts in two minutes."

"Oh yeah, right!" Brett replied. Jack rushed down the hall toward the breakroom before the door opened and narrowly avoided exposing his eavesdropping. He grabbed a cup of coffee and headed to the meeting, stopping a few feet before the conference room door, trying to compose himself. Once ready, he walked through the doorway with a somewhat forced smile.

"Hi everyone. Thanks for coming. It sounded a little noisy from the hallway, so let's all simmer down and get to it." Jack motioned for everyone to take their seats.

The room fell quiet as all eyes shifted toward Jack. Rob Watkins, Accelx's CTO, leaned forward, looking ready to unleash some criticism. But then he seemed to read the room and instead leaned back in the brushed nickel and gray linen conference room chair.

"Look, I know everyone is working extremely hard, and for that I am grateful." Jack took a long pause and tried to make eye contact with everyone at the table. "But here's the reality: we must change course quickly. The board didn't mince words in my last meeting with them."

"Wait a minute. We hit our revenue target, right?" Don Simpson, Accelx's long-time CFO, spoke casually from a reclined position, his intertwined fingers resting calmly at the crest of his belly.

"Yes, we did." Jack nodded solemnly. "But that's not enough. Remember, Gold's purchase was about expanding into new verticals. That's why the board wants us to land more strategic accounts—and make those accounts happy once we get them. Unfortunately, we're currently in the position of trying to save one of the three strategic accounts we have. I believe by now you're all aware of Onergize's feedback to the board, right?" Jack watched a few people nod and a few people shift in their seats. "It's time for us to get back on track—and fast."

"Well, I can tell you this, it's not a technology issue," said Rob, folding his arms across his chest. "We're ready to go."

"Actually, Rob," Hannah DeSantos, Accelx's Chief Operating Officer, interjected, "there are a few software challenges my team is working through. We should discuss. These tech glitches are challenging the user experience and annoying some key adopters at Onergize. I've been trying to get on your calendar about this for a couple of weeks."

"Okay, good, Hannah. Rob, I want you to meet with Hannah so the two of you can report on those challenges and give me a status update by the end of the day," Jack directed. "What else can you guys tell me about Onergize?"

"Honestly?" Hannah started. "Ops needs more resources to do these implementations. It's way more work than we thought it would be. I've pulled everyone on the team over to focus on this account. It's still not enough manpower, and I'm worried our existing customers are going to suffer."

"Okay, I want to understand this in more detail. We can't afford to lose any customers or have service for our current clients deteriorate. Schedule a meeting with me for tomorrow." After his comment to Hannah, Jack turned to face Brett. "Let's talk about sales. Any progress on the strategic account pipeline? Did your team follow up on the Radiance intro I made? They're an ideal strategic account target."

"Yeah, my team is talking to Radiance as we speak," Brett replied. "Also, the marketing firm just gave us some new sales decks for strategic accounts. I think these will be helpful for the team. But our lead gen is still light for strategic accounts. I met with a new firm that I'd like us to consider. Our existing firm can't seem to fill the pipeline enough."

"Our lead gen firm has always handled about half of the pipeline while cold calls by the sales team filled the other half. Are we changing our approach?" Don asked. "Last I checked, our firm was meeting quotas. We have a good working relationship with them. I'd hate to start over with a new firm."

"I think we need a different approach for strategic accounts." Brett leaned forward in his chair as he spoke. "I need my guys focused on closing in these new markets. Cold calls would be a distraction."

"It'd have to be cost neutral," Don replied with a frown on his face.

Brett continued, ignoring Don's comment. "I'd also like to reopen the discussion about letting the current bench of sales reps go. This just doesn't seem to be the team that can get it done."

Shauna's eyes shot up from her tablet. "Brett, we just talked about this! We're not going down this path again, at least not until both of us sit down with Jack and dissect the challenges your team is facing. Right now, there's no financial incentive for them to even try to land strategic accounts because they make plenty of money on existing verticals. Let's stop and think through what it looks like to hire top talent in a competitive market while battling a reputation for firing salespeople who have met their sales targets. Do you really think that's going to fly? I know that's a scenario I sure don't want to face."

"I think that's a little dramatic," Brett said sheepishly, looking at the table to avoid Shauna's irritated glare. "I just can't be successful with this team. I'm going to need to add resources to help us through this."

"Look, everyone, the answer can't always be more people and more resources," Don interjected. "I've got to watch the numbers carefully until we're back on track. We simply don't have the budget to spend willy-nilly. The board is all over me about cash flow, so we have to prioritize."

"There's nothing 'willy-nilly' about having the resources to service the few strategic accounts we have landed," Hannah asserted with a hint of desperation in her voice. "Ops can't be successful without additional investment."

"Well, wait a minute, Hannah, the sales team needs to be the priority right now," Brett interjected. "Remember, there's no ops without sales."

"Hold on, guys, I still need the technology upgrades we discussed before the end of the year, or tech will—" Rob started.

Brett cut him off. "With all due respect, Rob, there's no point in tech investments if sales are down."

"Okay, enough!" Jack snapped, raising his right hand and rubbing his forehead with his left. The group fell silent. Only the hum of the copy machine next door and the steady rhythm of keyboard clicks echoing from down the hall filled the void.

"Look," Jack began, "before we invest anything anywhere, each of us must make sure we're doing everything to close and service strategic accounts. This is the board's mandate—to grow these new verticals. It's why they acquired Accelx. End of story. I'd like each of you to set aside two hours for me next week to review your functions on a one-on-one basis. I don't want you to go crazy preparing stuff, but let's look at the basics and brainstorm about what's going well, where we need to improve, and what investments you think you'll need."

"Two hours?" Don rubbed the top of his shiny bald head. "Is that necessary for finance? I mean, we've been at this a long time, I'm not sure we can do more to contribute to the growth of the business."

Jack swerved his chair and looked directly into his CFO's eyes. "Yes, Don, it is absolutely necessary. I appreciate that we have a mature finance function, but each and every one of us must take a hard look at what we can be doing better. In today's competitive environment, companies either grow or die, so please reframe your mindset on growth." Jack surprised himself with his forceful delivery.

"Okay, sure, boss," Don said, shrugging.

Jack inhaled deeply, then centered his chair to face the entire team. "Thank you in advance for making the time. Dean will coordinate with each of your assistants, so please alert them to this priority. I want each of us to have an action plan in less than two weeks. First, we'll present to this group. Next, we'll refine and prioritize investments. Then, we'll present to the board when they are in town three weeks from now. That's all guys. Thanks. Let's get moving."

The team slowly pulled together their belongings and headed back to work. Jack stood up and glanced through the interior plate glass windows of the conference room.

"One more thing." Everyone froze, and Jack turned back to look at them. "I just want to say that I really believe in this team. You guys are the best and brightest out there, and I know we can turn this around."

Everyone mumbled a halfhearted thank-you and finished shuffling out of the room. Jack was the last to leave. As he exited the room, he nearly ran into Brett, who was waiting only inches outside the conference room door.

"Hey boss. Got a minute?"

CHAPTER 6

AS THEY EXITED the conference room, Jack motioned for Brett to follow him to his office. They walked in silence down the long corridor with only the echoes of their loafers on the gray vinyl plank floor and the hum of the copy machines to fill the void. Once they arrived, Jack motioned for Brett to take a seat. "So, what's up?" Jack asked as he set his tablet on the desk.

"Well, it's just that I was kind of surprised in the meeting. I thought you were going to talk to Shauna about the team changes we discussed?"

"I did. I've gotta say, Brett, she has raised some very good points." Jack settled into his office chair with a big post-meeting exhale. "She said she raised them with you, and you agreed."

"Like what?" Brett ran his fingers nervously through his hair.

"Like we didn't incentivize the team correctly, and you admitted you haven't given the team specific feedback on their performance."

Brett looked down at the vinyl plank floor and kicked it with his khaki loafer. "I knew you would take her side."

"Her side?" Jack was taken aback. "We're a team. There are no sides."

"Yeah, sure. But let's be honest, you *always* agree with her," Brett said. Jack could hear the irritation rising in his voice as he continued. "Just because she was a recommendation from Gold, you think she can do no wrong."

"C'mon. That's simply not true or fair." Jack sat up and leaned on the desk. "Let's talk about this."

"I'm sorry, boss, but I just don't see any other way to do this if I can't change out my team."

"Really? Are you sure you've exhausted every possibility?" Jack asked. "It would take a lot of time to build a new sales team—and time is one thing we don't have. The board was clear that we have only ninety days left to show measurable progress. New sales teams are a long-term play. We need short-term solutions right now. We have to figure out how to support and overcome challenges with the existing team. At least we know they can sell our product. That's huge!"

"Yeah, but they don't know the pharmaceutical and medical device industries." Brett shook his head. "I've spent so much time with them, and nothing has changed."

"I understand. Listen, let's carve out some time next week with Shauna to come up with some constructive feedback for each of your team members. Let's figure out how to get them on the right track. Remember, I worked with that team for a long time, so I have some perspective I can share too. This will also give Shauna an opportunity to dig deeper and understand the situation better."

"Fine," Brett said, his voice sounding like that of a pouty teen. "But I'm also going to start working my network for reps with experience in these new verticals. I'm sorry, but I just don't have the same confidence in our current team as you two do. And as I said in the meeting, sales investments must trump everything else."

Jack tried to hide his frustration with his longtime mentee. "As long as you don't lose focus on the short-term goal here. Your current team has to make *significant* progress on strategic accounts in the next ninety days. Are we clear on the importance of this goal?"

"Of course." Brett stood up. "Gotta run to a meeting with the team. Catch up later."

"Before you go, when can I expect the latest outreach metrics? I'm sure you remember my email about not receiving an update since January. You replied that I'd have them this week."

"Yeah, boss. Sorry, I'm on it. You'll have them by end of day today." Brett raced out of Jack's office.

Jack clicked on his calendar to see what was next. Realizing he had a ten-minute break, he pulled up his inbox to go through his emails. He was in the midst of responding to Shauna about an employee issue when he heard a light knock on the door.

"Hey." Don's round figure was standing in the doorframe. "Sorry, Dean wasn't at his desk, so I thought I'd just see if you had a quick moment to chat."

"Sure." Jack stood up and motioned for Don to meet him at the conference table. "What's up?"

"Look, you know I've been at this CFO thing a long time," Don started. "And I get what a big push going into new markets is, but we still have to be mindful of expenses. The team just seems to think we can spend, spend, spend. We must shore up our P&L if we're not hitting our strategic account targets, that's what the board will expect from us and from me as CFO—and trust me, it will buy us some time with them."

Jack rocked back and forth slightly in his chair for a moment, trying to reconcile Don's perspective with what he'd heard from the board. Guillermo was firm about what Jack needed to do, and he wasn't sure how they'd react if he missed his goals but came in with a strong P&L. The board seemed unimpressed by the fact that they'd met their revenue goals. They were hyperfocused on the fact that they'd missed their strategic account goals.

"Well, I think you made it clear we need to prioritize our investments in the meeting today," Jack replied, "and I support you on that. That's why we're having those two-hour meetings."

Don shook his head. "Yeah, but the rest of the team doesn't respect my position. Hannah is all over me about needing to hire more people, Brett's just looking for a quick fix no matter the cost, and Rob wants to keep buying the latest techy bells and whistles for himself. And I think we could give *all* our profit to Shauna and she'd still complain that we don't have enough HR investment. We can't operate this way. I have a responsibility to the board."

Jack took a deep breath. "You do, and I appreciate where you are coming from, but you also have a responsibility to enable the company's growth. We're going to have to figure something out here, because we can't cost cut our way to success."

"Tightening up the purse strings is exactly what we need to do right now," Don argued. "I'm telling you, it will buy us time with the board until the sales team can land more strategic accounts."

"I don't know." Jack leaned back in his chair and folded his arms across his chest. "The board was crystal clear with me about the ninety-day mandate. That's where I plan to focus my attention, and I'm going to need your support to help us prioritize investments."

"With all due respect, I think Brett's going to need more than ninety days to get the sales team focused on strategic accounts. You really need to think about how you can buy some time with the board." Don stood up to leave. "Trust me, I can help you navigate this. The investors go nuts for a financially disciplined business. Give it some thought."

Jack sat at the conference table and watched Don leave his office. He wasn't quite sure what to make of the exchange. After a few moments, he stood up and walked over to his office window to look out at the skyline. His head was throbbing again, but he fought the urge to pack up his stuff and finish the day at home. He rubbed his temples and tried to refocus on what he needed to do for the day.

"Jack?" Rob walked into his office. "Dean said it'd be okay for me to come in. Do you have a minute?"

Flustered, Jack reminded himself that he wanted to be a leader with an open-door policy. Of course some days, like today, his door felt like a subway turnstile. "Sure. Do you want to join me over here at the window? It's a nice day to take in the view, and I know you appreciate the Atlanta skyline."

Rob walked over and stood next to his boss. It was a bright spring day, with the light hitting the buildings and giving them a pleasant sheen.

"Yeah, it's quite a view," Rob observed.

Jack grinned. "What's up?"

"Well, I wanted to talk with you about Hannah. She seems to think the Onergize issues are all technology related, and I don't agree. We've tested the changes thoroughly. I feel strongly Onergize's frustrations are with ops issues, not tech issues."

Jack's grin faded, and he reluctantly motioned to the conference room table. He grabbed two small bottles of water from his mini fridge on the way over and tossed one to Rob, who caught it in his right hand.

"And you discussed this with Hannah?" Jack asked.

"Yeah, but I'm not getting anywhere." Rob took a sip of water. "She keeps insisting that I'm missing something. You know my tech is top-notch. You said the other day it's the competitive advantage that sets us apart."

Jack took a long swig of water, hoping it would provide some relief from his headache. "That's right, but it doesn't mean it's flawless."

"Of course," Rob acknowledged, "but Hannah isn't even willing to consider other possibilities. She's just pointing the finger at tech. I need you to talk to her. We can't stabilize Onergize if she won't look at the overall problem. I'm stuck."

"Okay, let me do some digging with her and see where she's at." Jack finished off his water and tossed the empty bottle into the recycle bin. "In the meantime, please continue to try to work with her. We have to figure this out—and fast. We simply can't lose the Onergize account."

"I'll try, boss." Rob stood up to leave. "Thanks for the talk. I'll see you this weekend?

"Yep, looking forward to it." Jack tried his best to sound enthusiastic.

After Rob left, Jack walked over to his desk, pulled open the top drawer, and searched until he found a bottle of painkillers. His head was now throbbing. He downed two pills, replaying the team meeting as well as the conversations with Brett, Don, and Rob in his head. *Guillermo was right. Something is definitely off with the team. How could Brett think I would take sides? Why does Don not believe in Brett? Why are Rob and Hannah fighting about Onergize? Why is everyone so focused on their own turf?*

He leaned back and rubbed his aching head. *Another day,* Jack thought, *and we're not a single step closer to meeting the board's ninety-day mandate.*

Jack sank down into his chair, closed his eyes, and let his head slump into the palms of his hands. He hoped the painkillers would kick in quickly.

"God my head hurts," he whispered to the empty room.

CHAPTER 7

TWO DAYS LATER, in unseasonable scorching heat, Jack stood in the back corner of Rob's brick patio, checking his phone to try to get a score of the preseason Atlanta United FC game. Unable to get any information, he shoved the phone back into his pocket, crossed his arms, and scanned the crowd at the party. His wife, Bridget, had been on him since last night about his mood, but he couldn't help it. The events of the past week kept playing in his head. A few moments earlier, he'd rubbed sunscreen all over Quinn and Jamie and fitted them with floaties on their chubby arms. He'd hovered over them while they splashed in the pool until Bridget shooed him away to go mingle with the group. He realized he didn't have the energy to socialize, so he found a quiet spot for some alone time.

"Brewsky?" Brett held a can of beer in Jack's face. "You look like you could use one."

Jack stared at the beer for a second before taking it, wondering if alcohol was a wise choice in his current frame of mind. Finally, he reached his hand out. "Yeah, what the heck," he said with a half smile. He cracked opened the beer and took a sip. The two men watched the older kids play Marco Polo in the pool while Jamie and Quinn waded around the shallow end under the watchful eye of Bridget.

Brett finally broke the silence. "Nice party. Can't believe Rob's little guy is seven years old. Seems like just yesterday when he was born. Time moves fast."

Jack nodded and took another sip of beer. He saw Jamie jump into the pool, his floaties keeping his little body and head atop the water. Jack caught Bridget's eye, and she mouthed, "Stop brooding." Jack shrugged and looked away.

"So, what's the score of the soccer game?" Brett took a sip of beer. "Your guys up today?"

"Since when do you care about soccer?" Jack faced Brett with a curious look on his face. "Thought you were a baseball guy."

"I am." Brett smiled. "But I know how much you care about your club."

Jack checked his phone again. "No updates. So frickin' annoying."

The two stood in silence and surveyed the crowd of approximately twenty people socializing in little groups around the yard. A few of Rob's friends were lingering by the barbecue with Rob, who was grilling burgers and hot dogs. Some folks had their feet in the pool, trying to cool off. The kids were all splashing around in the water without a care in the world.

"You okay, boss?" Brett asked. "You seem a little stressed."

Jack took a long sip of beer. "Just a little tired. Long week. Trying to shake it off, I guess."

"For what it's worth, I think the board was totally unfair to you. They don't have a clue about what it takes to penetrate these strategic markets. We're doing everything we can, don't they get that?"

Jack took a deep breath. "Look, don't take this the wrong way, but they're right."

"Nah, man, not you too," Brett started. "This shit takes time. You know that."

"I agree," Jack said, nodding. "But we've had fifteen months and the team's still not making progress. I'm starting to think we need to do something different here."

"Like what?" Brett took a sip of beer.

Jack contemplated what to say for a few moments. They were at a seven-year-old's birthday party, and he wanted to be respectful of Rob and his family. At the same time, he was frustrated and felt like a calm conversation with Brett as a friend could help him right now.

"Hey, let's go grab a seat over there." Jack pointed to a wooden bench that was under an impressive oak tree, which provided ample shade. "I'm tired of standing."

Brett followed Jack to the bench and sat down next to him.

"Brett, I want you to understand, we're on a short leash here. You're the leader, you're accountable. It's not okay to blame your team."

"I know that," Brett responded, somewhat defensively.

"Well, to be honest, you haven't been acting that way—not with me and not with Shauna. When I was in your role, I didn't blame you guys when things went wrong. I stepped up and figured out how to make it right. That's the job, and that's what you need to do now. You've got to own this."

"I do own this!" Brett countered. "I'm doing everything you're asking me to, but this shit's hard!"

"Of course it's hard." Jack shook his head. "If it were easy, anybody could do it. But we've asked you to do it because we think you've got what it takes. Don't prove us wrong. Honestly, you just seem unfocused."

"Unfocused?" Brett looked offended. "Give me an example."

"Well, for one thing, the outreach metrics you promised to send me every day this week. Why don't I have those yet?" Jack shot back.

"Ah, c'mon, man!" Brett dismissed. "I just haven't had a chance. I can't believe you're making such a big deal about one set of metrics. I'll send them as soon as I get home from the party. Honestly, I've got bigger things on my plate—like penetrating these new strategic markets. It's a totally different ballgame that you didn't have to deal with when you were CRO, so please cut me some slack!"

"Well, you're partially right. I've never had to enter new markets here at Accelx, but I have at other companies. Listen, I'm here to help, but I need you to step it up and work with me to right this ship and meet the board's ninety-day mandate. Time is not our friend."

Brett sat in silence for a moment, seemingly contemplating Jack's words. He drained the last of his beer and crushed the can.

"Look, I want to fix this more than anything," Brett started, "and I'm willing to do what it takes. But I do need some more support from you."

"Like what?" Jack asked.

"Like the lead gen stuff." Brett crossed his arms. "And I need more support with the sales team. Like real help."

"I'm open to the lead gen stuff," Jack said. "And we're already finding time to work through the feedback on the sales team with Shauna."

Brett shook his head. "No offense to Shauna, but HR crap is not going to solve this problem. We need real feedback."

"Brett, c'mon. Shauna's the real deal. She can really help if you let her."

"I'll think about it." Brett stood up. "You want another beer?"

"No, you go ahead." Jack shaded his eyes to look for his kids. "I'm going to check the score again and then relieve Bridget for a bit."

Brett took a few steps forward but then turned around and faced Jack. "You know, I'm grateful for everything you've done for me. The way you've taken me under your wing and supported me over these past several years by giving me all these opportunities—well, you kind of remind me of my dad. No one's done anything like this for me before."

"It's so unfair that he didn't live to see your success, buddy." Jack stood up and put his hand on Brett's shoulder. "From everything you've told me, it sounds like he was a phenomenal guy. I wish I could've met him."

"Me too." Brett smiled at Jack, then he turned around and continued walking.

Jack watched Brett make his way to the cooler and start chatting with a developer on Rob's team. He watched the two of them smiling and laughing and wondered if the gravity of his conversation with Brett had landed. Did Brett understand that something had to change, that his team would have to start operating differently and turn the ship around fast because it was headed for an iceberg? A feeling of dread washed over Jack. He pulled out his phone, but instead of checking on the game, he searched for Meg's email address.

Hi Meg,

Sorry to bother you on a Saturday. Any chance we could meet on Monday? I will make whatever availability you have work with my schedule.

Thanks,
Jack

CHAPTER 8

TWO DAYS LATER, Jack impatiently tapped his fingers on his desk while he waited to be let into the video conference. He glanced at his watch. The Atlanta sun was slowly sinking lower in the late afternoon sky and peeking through the window shade slats, casting long, thin shadows across his office. It was day four of a spring heat wave. He was grateful for the air-conditioning that kept his thirty-seventh-floor office at a perfect seventy degrees.

"Hi Jack," Meg greeted him once the video call window popped up. "Sorry I'm a few minutes late. My last meeting ran over. How was your weekend?"

"Hey Meg." Jack waved. "It was okay. It's unusually hot here this week. The kids managed to have a lot of pool time, but I must admit, I was pretty distracted. How was yours?"

"It was nice. Had a BBQ on Saturday with some friends. We're having good weather right now in LA, so no complaints. I wrote some poetry, which always restores me." Meg smiled.

"You write poetry?" Jack was surprised. "That's cool. Can I read some of it?"

"Yeah, I've written my whole life. Best way to clear my head. Happy to share some pieces with you, but fair warning, it's generally not feel-good stuff." Meg laughed, straightening in her chair. "Tell me what's going on. I was surprised to get your email on Saturday. It sounded urgent."

"It is, and I appreciate you making time for me so quickly." Jack picked up his soccer stress ball and squeezed it hard. "I had a team meeting last week that I can't stop thinking about."

"Okay, is that why you were distracted this weekend?"

"Yeah." Jack looked down at the stress ball compressed in his clenched hand. "I'm starting to think Guillermo is right. Something is off with my team."

"Okay, let's start with the team meeting. Tell me about it."

Jack put his stress ball down. "It was the first in-person leadership gathering we'd had since the board meeting last week, and I was shocked by everyone's reaction."

"Really? Tell me more."

"Everyone was talking *at* one another instead of *to* one another. I feel like they are each focused on their own stuff and think our problems are someone else's fault. They're all so defensive. And then, after the meeting, Brett accused me of taking sides with Shauna. Taking sides! What the hell is that supposed to mean? We're a team. There are no sides." He took a quick breath before rushing on. "Then, Don came in and tried to convince me that we should hold all spending to buy time with the board. A few minutes later, Rob popped in and dropped a bomb that he believes Hannah is trying to blame the tech team for her own ops problems with the Onergize implementation. Earlier this week, Shauna said I had a soft spot for Brett, which is ludicrous. What are we, in high school again or something? I basically hid from Hannah the rest of the week because I was afraid she was going to throw something at me too." Jack realized he was furiously squeezing his stress ball in front of the camera. "Sorry, I'm just really frustrated."

"It's okay." Meg took a long, slow sip of water from her water bottle. "Let's just step back for a moment and sort through all this. First off, let me be open. I know Shauna well from her previous company but haven't spoken to her about anything professional since she left."

"Renata mentioned that," Jack acknowledged. "And I let Shauna know we'd be meeting. She said the same thing."

"Good," Meg replied. "With that out of the way, let me ask you something."

"Sure," Jack replied.

"Who did you expect to take accountability for the current issues the company is facing?"

Jack rubbed the stubble on his chin as he thought. "Well, all of them, I guess. I mean, Brett should take accountability for his team's lack of performance, but he's blaming Shauna for not letting him fire everyone. And Hannah and Rob should have taken accountability for Onergize going rocky instead of blaming each other. Don needs to enable the growth of the company and believe in our team."

"Why do you think things didn't go as you expected?"

"I don't know." Jack shook his head. "I've been trying to figure that out all weekend." Jack wondered if the beads of sweat forming on his forehead were visible over video.

"Hmm." Meg straightened in her chair. "One follow-up question: How are you currently holding your team accountable?"

"By acquiring strategic accounts and servicing them, of course." Jack could feel the muscles in his neck tensing and wondered where this was going. "I thought that would be obvious?"

"Okay, let's start with Brett," Meg countered. "He hasn't acquired a single strategic account yet. When I've asked you about this, you've told me it takes time. What are you doing in the meantime to hold Brett accountable?"

"Well, I'm spending a ton of time with him. I'm helping him plan to get strategic accounts by giving him feedback and guidance. And this week, we're going to start figuring out how to coach his team."

"So, your focus is primarily on Brett—is that correct?" Meg smoothed her green-and-white gingham blouse. "Are you meeting with the other leaders on your team?"

"Yes, I have one-on-ones with them every week."

"And what do you talk about?"

"I let them guide the agenda—whatever issues are top of mind for them. They're strong leaders and have been in their roles for a while now. They know their areas best. I'm not sure I can add a lot more to help them." Jack exhaled loudly. "Meg, where are we going here? I feel like these are obvious questions."

"Are they? I'm sorry you feel that way. But I need to make sure I have the lay of the land from your perspective before providing mine. Let me see if I understand . . ." Meg tucked her blonde hair behind her ears and leaned forward. "You're holding Brett accountable for acquiring strategic accounts, but no one on the leadership team is seeing any progress. In the meantime, you're spending more and more time with Brett. And when you meet with individual leaders, you're letting them guide the agenda with their functional issues."

"Yes, yes," Jack agreed, barely hiding his irritation. "That's right."

"Indulge me for one more minute," Meg continued.

"Sure." Jack fought the desire to roll his eyes. He put down his soccer stress ball. "Go ahead."

Meg tilted her head to the side. "What message do you think your behavior is sending to your team?"

"What?" Jack wasn't even attempting to hide his exasperation now.

"You said you'd indulge me for another minute, so please do. What message do you think the team is taking away from your behavior?"

"Look, they know how to get things done. Hannah has been here as long as I have and can delight customers in her sleep. Rob knows this technology like the back of his hand, and he's the only one who could have modified the software to work for the new verticals in the given timeframe. Yes, there are minor annoyances here and there, but it will get back on track. My bigger issue is acquiring strategic accounts right now," Jack replied, emphasizing each word as if Meg might be having trouble hearing him.

"Jack, I understand exactly what you are saying." Meg leaned into the screen, also enunciating each word as she spoke. "What I think you are missing is how people are interpreting your behavior."

Jack's facial expression shifted to pure confusion.

Meg smiled slightly. "From what you've described, it feels like you are encouraging everyone to act within their own silos and not look at the bigger picture."

"Sorry, but that's ridiculous," Jack pushed back, though less defensively. "Everyone knows they are accountable for delivering on strategic accounts. That's the whole thesis of the Gold investment."

"Sure," Meg responded, "and in their own minds, they each feel they are delivering on strategic accounts within their own functions. It may even be true. But is this siloed approach preventing you and your executive team from achieving the overall company goals together?"

"I'm not sure I follow," Jack said. "They are all incentivized to achieve the company's goals. It's part of their bonus."

"Yes, but right now, you're reacting to each and every problem at the functional level but failing to encourage them to work together as a cohesive unit to achieve the company's strategic goals *together*. Your team isn't aligned, and it sounds like they spend most of their time advocating for their own functions and performance over the needs of the team and the company."

Jack ran both of his hands through his sandy-blond hair and sat back in his chair. He was silent for a moment, reflecting on Meg's statement.

"And that's why Brett is all over Shauna, why Hannah and Rob are battling each other, and why Don is basically frustrated with everyone?" Jack shook his head in response to his own rhetorical question.

"Look," Meg started slowly, "it's like I said last week—teams need to be led toward a goal and aligned on the plays to execute and achieve that goal together. In my thirty years of experience, I've never seen a leadership team succeed unless the CEO has been intentional about alignment. It's time to start building bridges between these departmental fiefdoms."

"Okay, okay, I'm starting to get your point," Jack said, nodding. "And I agree that maybe I'm reacting to everyone at a functional level. But each of these problems is something that needs fixing at a functional level. I need everyone on this team to do their damn jobs!"

"But that's exactly why you need to step in and lead your team at a higher level, at a strategic level, a company level." Meg placed both hands flat on her desk as she spoke. "Every company has finite resources, and members of the leadership team often vie for those resources without considering what the company actually needs to achieve its goals. But when you have alignment, leaders willingly share resources to help the company achieve its goal—even as they still advocate for what they need. They collaborate, cooperate, and work together toward shared goals. Does that make sense?"

"Yes. I'm think I'm getting it now. They will act more like a cohesive unit if there's alignment." Jack scribbled a note on his tablet. "And you think that's why we're struggling? So, instead of listening to them at a functional level, I need to start guiding them to think more at the team and company level, right?"

"Yes, I think this is one of the places where you're struggling." Meg smiled encouragingly. "We'll have to dig deeper to see what else is going on."

"Okay, I admit it. This is helpful . . . yes, very helpful." Jack smiled back, feeling the tension in his neck release a bit. "But where do we start?"

"We'll start by defining clear, one-year goals that encompass the ninety-day mandate the board gave you for your team." Meg folded her hands and placed them in her lap. "Everyone needs to understand the importance of these goals and what they need to do to help the team and the company achieve them. Everyone needs to get laser focused on the right things—and you're going to make those clear to everyone. They also need to be inspired.

Your message must be more than 'acquire strategic accounts.'" Meg deepened her tone to that of a gruff male and waved her pointer finger as she spoke, which made Jack laugh. "I want you to really think about where Accelx needs to be in one year and create a picture of what that looks and feels like. We'll work together to figure out how to articulate this in a compelling way. Sound like a plan?"

"Okay, yeah." Jack nodded enthusiastically. "I'll do some thinking on this. Could we set up another meeting some time on Thursday or Friday, if that works for your schedule?"

"Sounds great. Looking forward to it. Bye for now." Meg waved as she ended the meeting.

Jack stood up and placed his hands on the back of his neck. He pushed his elbows back for a good long stretch and thought, *What will Accelx look like one year from now if we achieve our goals?*

"It's a very good question," he said out loud.

CHAPTER 9

THE NEXT MORNING, Jack heard the front door shut from his second-story home office as Bridget left to take the kids to daycare before heading to her office. It had taken quite a bit of shuffling, but the night before, Jack had managed to clear his schedule to focus on figuring out what Accelx would look like one year from now. He told his assistant, Dean, not to interrupt him under any circumstances. He shuddered to think what his email would look like by the end of the day. *Nothing I can* *do about that right now,* he thought and pushed the sentiment out of his mind.

Suddenly, everything was perfectly still and quiet, except for the ticking grandfather clock in the corner. *Time just never slows down, does it?* He pulled his tablet from his brown leather bag and opened the notes app to a blank page. The first thoughts that came to him had nothing to do with work.

In one year, Jamie will be in in kindergarten and Quinn will finally be playing soccer. She'll be the best three-year-old forward in the league. That power! She's a rock star.

A wide smile spread across his face, but it quickly faded as he picked up his stylus and stared at the blank page that cried out for information about the one-year vision for Accelx. He cracked his neck and rolled his shoulders, trying to get in the right frame of mind for the task at hand.

We need enough strategic accounts to demonstrate to the board that we can get into these new markets. They said within 25 percent of our revenue target. So how many more strategic accounts would we need to hit that target?

Jack walked over to the soccer ball he kept in his office and started dribbling it across the wooden floor. Bridget was always on his case about not doing this in the house, but she wasn't home, and it helped him think.

Brett's going to throw out some crazy number like twenty. That would definitely show the board, but there's no way we can hit that. We've got to be realistic about what we can do and what the organization can handle. And I can't be the one who closes these accounts, so people are going to need more training. Time. Yep, that's going to take time.

He lightly kicked the ball through the open door of his office. "And he scores!" he exclaimed, mimicking the cheers of jubilant spectators.

And then there's the issue of Brett and his team. I thought he'd done better with managing his team over the past year or so . . . but those outreach metrics he finally sent me were incomplete. How could he not know his team was so unfocused? Why didn't he give them any performance feedback?

He retrieved the ball from the hall and dribbled it over to his desk. *I know everyone's busy, but that makes no sense. It'd be one thing if he were closing strategic accounts and neglected the team. But nothing seems to be getting done. What's happening there?*

Leaving the soccer ball under his desk, Jack started pacing back and forth.

Maybe Shauna has a point. I need to do some more digging. Maybe I just need to be more hands-on to bridge this gap. Shit, I've got to fix this—and fast!

Realizing he was getting a bit worked up, he said, "Okay, okay," out loud before inhaling slowly and deeply. "You've got this."

Okay, I could bring Brett and the sales reps together for some team building. I could pump everyone up and get them aligned around strategic accounts. There's still time, but I've gotta come up with something soon. He picked up the tablet from his desk to capture his thoughts.

After we hit our ninety-day mandate, we shoot for three more strategic accounts in six months. That would chill out the board and get us within 10 percent of our revenue target, assuming those accounts are the right size. From there, we'll hit a stride and end the year on target.

But that wasn't all that needed doing. "Onergize," he whispered under his breath.

Maybe Hannah and I should meet with their CEO directly and assure him we're all over this. That should put them at ease and allow me to hear some of his concerns firsthand to get a better understanding of the core problem. And that would help me manage Rob's concerns too without having to be a go-between for Rob and Hannah.

He sat down at his computer and typed an email to Meg with his goals, also asking if she had some time to talk tomorrow.

CHAPTER 10

"SO, WHAT DO you think?" Jack stared at the monitor, waiting for Meg's reaction like a kid waiting to open his first birthday present.

It had been three days since Jack's last meeting with Meg. The hot afternoon sun was peeking through the cracks of the closed blinds in his office. While Atlanta had enjoyed a brief reprieve from its heat wave yesterday, it had come steaming back with a vengeance this Thursday morning. Even though he loved to watch Jamie play soccer, he was dreading the sweaty experience scheduled for this afternoon.

"Okay." Meg looked up from her tablet, where she'd been scribbling notes. "Tell me more about the strategic account goal."

"Sure." Jack sat up in his chair. "I think if we can hit a good stride in six months, it'd fully restore the board's confidence in us, and we'd learn enough about these accounts to be able to execute at a much faster pace at the back end of the year and into early next year."

"Makes sense. It's a good start. So, what about—"

"Sorry to interrupt," Jack said excitedly. "But I also wanted to share that going through this process was *really* helpful. I realized I've gotta do some things differently with the team."

"Well, that's good to hear. Like what?"

"To start with, I have to step in and close this gap between Brett and his team. They need to get the right performance feedback as soon as possible, and I need to get the entire sales team aligned around closing these strategic accounts."

"Interesting . . ." Meg leaned forward. "Isn't that Brett's role?"

Jack took a sip of water. "Yeah, but I think he needs my help in getting this done—you know, like I need to model how to do it so he knows what to do going forward."

"And that doesn't raise any red flags for you?"

Jack was perplexed. "I don't follow. Isn't this my job?"

Meg rolled up the sleeves of her chambray shirt. "Actually no, it's Brett's job."

Jack snatched the stress ball off his desk and quietly pumped it several times. "Of course it is. I just mean that this is hard. There's no recipe book for selling into a new vertical. We need to give Brett some breathing room to figure this out."

"It's been fifteen months," Meg argued gently. "He's had a lot of breathing room. Let's unpack this a bit. First—and I see this all too often—companies choose executives based on their past successes. But this doesn't mean the person is automatically prepared to be successful in their new position." She shrugged. "There's just a general assumption that successful professionals will continue to be successful, no matter the role. It's actually really unfair, because there are often ability gaps that aren't addressed."

"That's true."

"Another thing we should discuss is what people perceive as your 'soft spot' for Brett. I don't know that I agree with their assessment. I think you're a very loyal professional, which is a good trait. But in this case, maybe you're being too loyal and a little overly protective of Brett."

"Overly protective?"

"Well, when you were the CRO, Brett worked as your deputy for a long time. Have you ever considered that you still might be leading Brett as a CRO instead of a CEO? Are you sure you're helping him learn to lead others toward success and not snatching the ball from him to run with it yourself?"

"I wouldn't ever try to take the ball from Brett—never. That's . . . that's just not how I operate," Jack stammered.

Meg sat perfectly still in her chair. Jack focused on the hum of the computer in his office, his eyes closing as he digested what she'd said.

Then his eyes shot open. "Shit, Meg! *Am* I trying to snatch the ball from Brett?"

"I don't think you're intentionally doing this; I just think it's a force of habit. You're just doing your job—but you're doing your old job, not your new one. Don't worry, we can work through this." Meg glanced back at her tablet. "Let's keep going. Okay . . . you've covered your strategic accounts goal. Good work. What else did you come up with?"

"Well, Hannah and I are meeting next week with the CEO of Onergize to personally assure him that we're all over this."

"Okay, that's a start. How about your one-year vision for Accelx?" Meg asked.

Jack's brow furrowed, and he felt like Meg had just taken back his birthday present. "Not sure I follow, Meg."

"Well, the assignment was to create a vision of what Accelx would look like in one year. You've outlined the number of strategic accounts you want—which is a good start—but it's only one piece of the puzzle." She gave Jack an encouraging smile. "What is your vision for the company with more strategic accounts? What does that look like for the rest of the organization? Again, your vision needs to be as the CEO, not CRO. Make sense?"

Jack stared at Meg, wide-eyed. "Uh . . . yes, okay. Well, to be honest . . . I thought the strategic accounts *were* the vision."

Meg raised her eyebrows. "That may have been the assignment when you were CRO, but—" Meg interrupted herself. "Jack, are you starting to see a pattern here? Your job is to paint a vision for the entire company, not just the sales team."

Jack rubbed his head. "Yeah, I'm starting to see it. I did actually start with the vision. I really did . . . I mean, I even threw out a ridiculously high number of strategic accounts and rationalized that we couldn't reach for that goal because of the implications for the rest of the organization."

"So, what went wrong?"

"I'm not sure." Jack offered a boyish grin and shrugged.

"It's okay. This is new, and it's a process." Meg smiled. "I know there's been a lot of pressure to land strategic accounts, which makes it the obvious focus area. But you need to figure out what all of this means for the rest of the organization. What will ops, product, finance, and even HR look like twelve months from now? Remember, your Onergize problem happened *after* you acquired them as a strategic account. Once you land these accounts, you've got to keep them happy and growing. That needs to be part of the vision."

Jack dropped his head into his hands and sat quietly for a few moments.

"You okay?" Meg asked, the concern clear in her voice.

Jack looked up with a tired smile. "Yeah, I'm okay. Truth is, I'm just not sure I know what my strategic vision is for the whole company yet. I still don't have a good grasp on all their functions, and I'm struggling to understand why. I mean, I've interacted with these teams for years, so I get the basics." He hesitated before continuing. "But it's different now that I'm the CEO. I'm going through these two-hour meetings with each of them and there is a lot of information, but I can't really say I'm taking away much."

"Mmm . . . that's not good. Why do you think you feel this way? Did you ask clarifying questions?" Meg leaned toward the screen.

"I did," Jack replied, shaking his head. "Tons of them, but their answers weren't crisp. It's like we're speaking different languages."

"Is it possible you *were* speaking two different languages?" Meg asked. "You know, back when I was just starting out as a leader, I often made the mistake of bringing to meetings metrics that were important to me and my function instead of bringing metrics that mattered to executives."

"What?" Jack sat up in his chair. "You made a mistake? Impossible!"

"Many actually!" Meg laughed. "I remember during one instance, the CEO asked me for an update on talent acquisition and I thought, *Woo-hoo, he's finally interested.* I spent an inordinate amount of time creating slides with trends on metrics like time to fill and aging requisitions, and I was so excited to share the deck with him. Imagine my surprise when he glanced at the slides for a second and then put them aside."

"I'd probably do the same thing if Shauna brought those to me," Jack admitted. "I'm sure they mean something to her, but what do I do with them?"

"Exactly," Meg emphasized. "High performing functional leaders know they have to connect these metrics to the business to be meaningful, but many, even at the top of the company, get stuck on only thinking about their function. If I had connected time to fill to impact to revenue and aging requisitions to customer satisfaction, I would have definitely gotten his attention."

"For sure." Jack sat back in his chair and rubbed his chin. "I definitely can see this being the case with Rob, maybe even Hannah sometimes. I need to think about the others. But I think this is only part of the challenge with those meetings."

"Okay, how did you set up these meetings? Did you have an agenda? Did you give them specific things to prepare before these meetings?"

"No, not really." Jack exhaled loudly, mostly because he was frustrated with himself. "I just wanted to have a conversation, to be respectful of their time. I'm not sure I can offer them a lot at this point. They're senior and so busy doing their day-to-day work. I just wanted to brainstorm about what we needed to meet the board's mandate. This always worked with the sales team when we were falling behind on our metrics." Watching Meg's reaction to his words, he said, "I can tell by the look you're giving me that you don't think it translates."

"Yep." They both laughed. "But seriously, why do you think that is? Why doesn't it translate?"

Jack folded his hands and put them on his desk. "I don't know."

"You seem a bit defeated?"

"Not defeated, just tired and a bit exasperated. Sometimes, it feels like you're answering all my questions with more questions, that's all."

Meg chuckled. "You know I don't have the answers. I just have clarifying questions to help you think through the answers yourself."

"Yeah, I'm starting to get that now. But it doesn't mean it's not frustrating."

"Touché." Meg put her hand on her heart like she'd been attacked. "But I promise we'll get there. Just be patient. I'm just concerned you're trying to run the plays that worked in sales across the whole company—and you're running a lot of those plays by yourself. Then, you're getting frustrated that you don't have the information you need from your team to do your job effectively as the CEO." She smiled. "I can see how that would be exhausting."

"Yeah, I'm not gonna lie, I'm pretty wiped out. I'm using the plays that have worked well for me throughout my entire career. But maybe you're right, maybe I need new plays."

"Think about it. Most sports teams create new plays every time new talent is added or they face a new competitor, right?" Meg took a sip of water. "It's no different in the business world. You've got to come up with new ways of working with your leadership team. Maybe ask them to build a simple maturity curve to see where they see their functions impacting the business today versus how they will mature over the next three to five years. I know Shauna appreciated the value of this exercise when we worked through these types of issues in her past job.

So maybe start with her?" she suggested. "Then, you could give feedback and have a discussion about how each of your teams' views align with Accelx's strategic growth. Even though they're senior talent, it's your job to lead them to achieve the vision you're painting for the company."

"I like that . . . it makes sense." Jack nodded. "And you're right—I think Shauna has one drafted, and we've just never found the time to really go through. But are you sure it doesn't feel like micromanaging?"

"It's interesting you ask that," Meg said, smiling. "The only person I'm worried about you micromanaging is Brett. For the rest of the team, no worries—they're expecting this from their CEO."

"Maybe you're right," Jack said. "I like the maturity curve approach. I'll get on it right away. I don't want to lose any more time. I think understanding a bit more about each leader's function will give me the insights I need to craft my one-year vision."

"Sounds good. Listen, I know this wasn't an easy session, but I think it was productive. I hope you agree." Meg made a note on her tablet. "If you need to chat before our next meeting, just shoot me a text and we'll jump on a quick call."

"Thanks, Meg. Yeah, it was hard but good. I think I'm starting to see what I need to do here." Jack waved and disconnected from the video call, his head spinning as he processed everything. He picked up his phone and texted Shauna to schedule time to review her maturity curve.

CHAPTER 11

IT'S BEEN A long time since we've done this," Hannah said, raising her stemless wineglass.

"Yes, cheers!" Jack grinned and raised his whiskey glass. "Things have been busy."

"For sure." Hannah took a sip of her cabernet sauvignon and placed her glass down on the wrought iron table. "I can't remember the last time we all got together. Maybe when we adopted Chico? Gosh, that was almost eighteen months ago."

Jack chuckled and surveyed the outdoor patio where they were enjoying a late afternoon drink before meeting their spouses at a nearby restaurant for dinner. Even though it was only 4:30 p.m., the patio bar was quite crowded for a Thursday afternoon. The heat wave of last week had subsided, leaving a mild breeze and moderate temperatures. It was downright pleasant to spend time outside.

"Yeah, Chico's a force!" Jack shook his head, thinking about the last time he saw the eighty-pound brown-and-black beauty fervently guarding the DeSantos's backyard. "How are the kids?"

"Ay, they're not little niños anymore. Jorge Jr. is struggling to write his college application essays. And Sienna is trying out for cheerleading." Hannah shook her head. "Growing up so fast!"

Jack nodded. "Well, it's great to catch up in person. I've missed having a drink with you and shooting the breeze. And I'm looking forward to dinner tonight. I feel like we haven't seen Jorge since the Gold acquisition."

"Yeah, it's been quite hectic. I'm looking forward to seeing Bridget too." Hannah took a sip of wine. "How are you holding up, Mr. CEO? I imagine the pressure must be unrelenting."

Jack took a long sip of whiskey and contemplated his answer. He studied the waiter as he served another round of drinks to a couple who were starting to get into an animated discussion at a corner table.

"Jack?" Hannah waved her hand in front of his eyes.

"Ugh, sorry!" Jack shifted his attention back to Hannah. "Yeah, it's tough, but we have a good team. I'm confident we will get there."

"That sounds like the party line." Hannah gave Jack the side-eye.

"No, it's the truth," Jack insisted, though maybe a bit too quickly. "I do believe in the team and our ability to lead Accelx to success. Actually, the sales team had some promising conversations with potential strategic accounts this week, so I'm feeling optimistic. I know we have a lot of work to do—that I have a lot of work to do, but . . . Did I mention I started working with a coach? It's been really helpful."

"Yeah, you said something about it when we started working on the maturity curve, which I thought was a good idea." Hannah tugged at the end of her long brown ponytail and watched the animated couple for a bit.

"But?" Jack asked.

"But what?" Hannah shifted her focus to trace the woven pattern on the wrought iron table with her right index finger.

"C'mon, Hannah," Jack prodded. "Don't beat around the bush. We've worked together a long time. Just tell me what you're thinking. Do you feel like we're *not* going to be successful?"

"It's not that." Hannah finished the last of her wine and signaled the waiter. "You okay with another round?"

"Sure!" Jack took the last sip of his whiskey and smiled. "If it's going to make you talk."

Hannah laughed. When the waiter stopped by a few moments later, she ordered another round of drinks and an order of buffalo wings to share.

"Have you had the wings here?" Hannah asked. "I'm not really a wings person, but the ones here are to die for. We come here for happy hour once a month just to devour a plate of them."

"I haven't." Jack unbuttoned his charcoal gray shirtsleeve and started to roll it up. "I'm excited to try them. You know I love me some wings."

Hannah smiled. "I remember!"

They both sat in silence, observing the growing activity on the patio. The tables were spaced out by six feet on each side to give the patrons a little privacy, and suddenly there wasn't an empty table to be seen.

"I guess you're not the only one who discovered the wings!" Jack laughed. "This place is packed."

Hannah laughed, then her face took on a serious look. "Thanks again for joining the meeting tomorrow with Onergize. I think our plan is solid. They've been much more responsive over the past few weeks, which is great, so I'm confident we'll be back on track soon."

"Glad to hear it and happy to join." Jack played with the lined edge of his napkin. "I hope Bernard shows. I would love to just talk to him, CEO to CEO, and assure him a bit."

Hannah nodded just as the waiter came by with their drinks, wings, sauce, plates, utensils, and extra napkins. After he arranged everything on the table, Hannah and Jack dug into the wings and ate in silence for a few moments.

"Oh man, I'm in heaven." Jack wiped his messy fingers on a paper napkin. "These are amazing!"

"Told you!" Hannah laughed and took a small sip of wine. "Go easy, though, you don't want to ruin your appetite."

"Ah, c'mon, you know Bridget always picks out a froufrou place that serves two pieces of shrimp as a main dish. I'll be okay." Jack crumpled up the orange-soaked napkin and placed it on the side of his plate. "So, look, you never answered my question. Be honest, do you have doubts about our ability to be successful?"

Hannah took a bite of a wing and seemed to chew at an excruciatingly slow pace, causing Jack to wonder if she was stalling.

"All I know is that Don's on my ass constantly about how much I'm spending," Hannah started. "He acts like I'm out on a shopping spree with his personal money. It's ridiculous."

"What do you mean?" Jack leaned back in his chair. "You're not over budget, are you?"

"No, everything's within my budget. He's just looking for ways to make his own metrics look good." Hannah exhaled. "Look, I am trying my best to get Onergize on track, but I feel like the finance team is a constant roadblock. His team even had the gall to suggest I cut a few of the resources, since we're not acquiring strategic accounts at the pace we thought, and maybe rehire them later."

"What? That makes no sense." Jack felt his blood pressure rising but forced himself to stay calm. "Are you sure you didn't mishear this?"

"No, I totally reamed Deidre, my finance resource, who suggested it." Hannah shook her head and served herself another wing. "It's like they have no concept of what we're trying to do."

"Have you spoken to Don about it?" Jack also served himself another wing and took a big bite.

"*Dios mio.*" Hannah rolled her eyes. "I've tried, I get nowhere! He reminds me that *he's* the one who answers to the investors and that if finance doesn't have their ducks in a row, Gold will lose confidence and then we'll be out on the street. He only listens to you."

"C'mon, Hannah." Jack wiped his mouth with a new napkin. "I know he can be difficult, but he is open to reason."

"He's open to *your* reason, not mine or anyone else's. Look, you asked. The only way I can get him to listen is by coming to you and having you swing the hammer. Otherwise, I'm wasting my breath."

Jack took a long sip of his second whiskey.

"Listen, I'm going to use the ladies' room before we head to the restaurant." Hannah stood up from the table and swung her purse on her shoulder. "We can walk. I checked the directions, and it's just two blocks away."

Jack nodded and watched Hannah navigate the patio crowd and make her way inside. He rubbed his forehead. *Brett. Shauna. Don. Hannah. Rob. They all play nice with me but attack one another. They're all working against one another. Meg's right, we've got to get more aligned.* He sighed and took out his phone to check his email. A message from Caroline Sweeting, CEO of Radiance, popped up.

> *Jack,*
>
> *I'm not sure what happened here, but it seems like we're stalled on the contract. Radiance remains interested in Accelx's services based on the conversations you and I had a few weeks ago. Can we talk soon?*
>
> *Caroline*

CHAPTER 12

THE NEXT DAY, Jack sat at his desk, rapidly editing the Radiance contract on his laptop, smoothing out some of the language based on his discussion with Caroline. She'd assured Jack she would sign the revised contract as soon as she received it. He made his last edit and hit send.

Though livid, Jack leaned back in his chair, hands folded behind his head. He turned to look out his office window. The fading sun coming through the glass warmed his face. He closed his eyes and basked in it for a moment—he could practically smell the daffodils blooming. He opened his eyes and glanced at his watch. Brett was a few minutes late. He shook his head.

A light knock on his office door made Jack turn around.

"Boss?" Brett asked. "Sorry I'm late. My team meeting ran over."

"Have a seat." Jack gestured to the conference table in his office. He grabbed two bottles of water from his mini fridge.

"Thanks." Brett took the water bottle from Jack's hand and sat down at the conference table. "I heard Radiance is going to sign today."

"Yes." Jack made himself comfortable in the chair across from Brett. "I sent Caroline the final contract, so we should have it back before the end of the day."

Brett nodded. "Do you think it will give us some breathing room from the board?"

"Not exactly." Jack folded his hands on the table. "That's what I wanted to talk to you about. Help me understand what happened with Radiance."

Brett sat quietly, seeming to intently study the vinyl plank floor below his chair. Jack intentionally did not break the uncomfortable silence.

Finally, Brett exhaled loudly. "I'm not exactly sure. Josie was working it, but then Radiance stopped responding, so she focused her attention on other accounts."

Jack unscrewed the cap of the water bottle and took a gulp.

"Did she escalate this to you?" Jack asked, playing with the small white cap.

"No. After you asked about it last week, I went to her, and she told me what was going on. I tried to call both our contact there and Caroline, but no one returned my calls."

"Did you ask Josie why she didn't escalate this? Surely, she knows our goal of acquiring strategic accounts?"

"I did." Brett nodded. "Josie said she prioritizes accounts that are active and responding."

"And what about you?" Jack asked. "I handed you a warm, qualified lead. Were you following up with Josie to get this done?"

"I've been fully focused on meeting lead gen firm replacements, which is also critical to driving strategic accounts." Brett shook his head. "I honestly just lost sight of this."

"Unfortunately, that's not good enough. I basically handed you guys this one and you couldn't get it done. Brett, you have to be able to focus on short- and long-term goals at the same time."

"I'm not sure what you expect me to say." Brett looked down. "I've been doing everything I can, working tons of hours. I told you this wasn't the right team to penetrate new markets, but you and Shauna won't let me make changes."

Jack took a deep breath and gathered his thoughts. "Look, we're on your side. Both Shauna and I are trying to coach you about how to communicate and work with your team. There was some direct engagement feedback in the last survey that indicated you still need to gain the confidence of your team—and that's after sixteen months on the job. Every time we try to give you specific ideas, you get defensive and tell us we don't understand. Your default response is to fire your entire team. Nothing is changing, Brett. Nothing is moving forward."

Brett shifted in his seat, his face flushed.

"When we worked together in sales, you were always open to feedback," Jack continued. "But something's different now. Why won't you accept any help to effectively lead your team?"

"When you were the CRO, you gave helpful feedback!" Brett responded angrily. Then he sighed and closed his eyes. "Now you and Shauna just give me this high-level stuff, which isn't helpful. This is not the team that can deliver what you're asking. They don't listen."

"Yes, but now you're the CRO, and it's your job to figure out how to get them to listen." Jack felt his blood pressure rising and quickly willed himself to calm down. "You should have been all over Radiance and Josie to make sure that deal got done. It's like you don't hold yourself as accountable for strategic accounts."

"That's not true!" Brett argued. "I've been trying so hard, even doing my own cold outreach. It's really, really hard."

Jack sat back in his chair and turned his head to look out the window. How he wished he could be out there right now, soaking up more sun, smelling all the blooming daffodils, and walking under the shade of the cherry blossom trees. He took a few slow breaths before continuing.

"Brett, I know this is hard." Jack leaned forward in his chair. "But this is the objective you have. It's been sixteen months, and we have yet to see progress. I have to ask, do you think you can do what we're asking you to do?"

They both let Jack's question linger in the air for a few moments. Brett leaned forward and took a sip of water, seemingly still contemplating his answer.

"I'm trying my best." Brett looked like a small child. "I really am."

"I know you are." Jack tried to make eye contact with Brett. "But your team's not making progress on strategic accounts, and that means we're not meeting the board's ninety-day mandate. At this point, I must consider other options, which may include bringing in a different leader. I'm not sure if it would be a fractional leader to work alongside you and the team and provide you with some focused help, or if it would be a more permanent solution."

"I see," Brett replied in a whisper.

"I'm sorry," Jack said gently. "I don't have a choice here, and I didn't want you to hear this from someone else."

Brett stared at the office wall with a blank look on his face. Finally, he took a deep breath. "Am I being fired?"

"Not yet," Jack replied. "But things can't continue like this. We have to make progress or Gold will lose confidence in us."

CHAPTER 13

FOUR DAYS LATER, Jack was watching dense raindrops pour down the outside of his home office window as he talked with Meg. "And as if all that weren't enough," he continued, "I met with Brett and Shauna yesterday to discuss coaching the sales team for the millionth time, and the two of them kept getting into it. I felt like a referee."

"How were they getting into it?" Meg inquired.

"Brett started off okay, but at some point, he just started to refute everything she said. He kept saying she couldn't possibly understand because she'd never been a sales leader. She eventually got annoyed and told him she didn't need to be in sales to help him work through a leadership problem. This infuriated Brett because he thought she was calling him a bad leader. I kept trying to calm them both down, but we didn't make much progress." Jack sighed. "After the meeting, Brett came to my office sulking about how he couldn't be successful while being handcuffed by HR. And just after he walked out, I had to field a call from Shauna, who told me I didn't support her in the meeting. It's like I'm their punching bag! They're both behaving like children, not leaders."

"Ugh, that's tough." Meg took a sip of green tea and carefully replaced the beige mug on the coaster on her desk.

"Yeah, this isn't what I imagined being CEO would be like. I've got to find a better way. We don't have a chance at success in our current state."

Tired and frustrated, Jack fell quiet and listened to the deluge of rain and the faint echo of his kids playing downstairs. He glanced at the grandfather clock in the corner of the room, a family heirloom that had once adorned his maternal great-grandparents' home. He cherished it, but at times he resented the constant reminder that time was always ticking away.

Meg broke the silence. "So, what are you thinking?"

"Honestly?" He grinned. "I just realized I'm going to need to start dinner right after this call. Sorry, it's been a crazy week. On top of the work crap, Bridget's been traveling for work, so I've got my hands full."

Meg smiled back empathetically. "Making anything good tonight?"

"A single malt, neat!" Jack laughed. "I wish, but I've got dad duty. I'm doing a chicken dish. Bridget will be home for dinner, and I'm sure she'd like something light and healthy after four days of being on the road and eating out."

"You're a good husband." Meg smiled as she took another sip of her tea.

"I try, but I know I make mistakes." Jack frowned. "Just like with this job."

"Hey, no one's perfect," Meg replied. "Mistakes are how we learn. Don't beat yourself up."

"I guess." Jack rubbed his right eye. "I just feel like you warned me about all this team dynamic stuff in our first call, and I was so adamant that it wasn't happening on *my* team. But it is, so I need to be more aware and intentional going forward. I need a new approach."

"It's great that you're now aware you need to do something different," Meg said. "It's progress. How did it go when you presented your one-year picture to the team?"

"Well, in theory, they all agreed it was crystal clear. But these last few weeks have taught me not to take things at face value. The problem is old habits die hard." He sighed. "I'm still not sure Don gets that he acts like a finance czar. And Rob just wants to dabble in the technology and code all day. And despite all my efforts with Brett, I'm still the only one closing all the strategic accounts!" Jack rubbed his forehead. "Sorry, I'm just exhausted. I'm burning the candle at both ends and don't know how much longer I can keep this up."

Jack looked away to try to compose himself and appreciated Meg's momentary silence. Though he wasn't looking at the computer screen, he could sense she was studying him.

"Look," Meg started in a quiet, gentle tone. "I get it. Anyone carrying the load you're carrying would be tired." She stopped and took a long sip of her tea. "But I have to be honest, your leadership style has in no small part contributed to your team's dysfunction, and the problem has been building for the last sixteen months. Now, it's spilling out all over the place."

"Well, thanks for not sugarcoating it." Jack rubbed the back of his neck.

"Do you want me to?" Meg smiled sadly. "I know it's hard to hear, but if you're being honest with yourself, you know it already, right? I'm pretty sure that's why you're so frustrated. You're upset with yourself. I'm just articulating your thoughts."

Jack closed his eyes and nodded his head. "So, I guess I can't just tell my team to grow the hell up?"

"Ha! Wouldn't that be nice," Meg laughed. "No, but it's time for some grown-up talk. You need to be crystal clear about your expectations. You need to lay down ground rules and hold people accountable—even yourself. No more enabling bad behavior on your team; cut it off at the knees."

"I might not have been clear," Jack argued, "but I don't believe I was enabling bad behavior. I'm not sure that's fair."

"Jack, really?" she said, intensifying her tone. "You let yourself play go-between for Brett and Shauna over and over. You've made it okay for everyone to come to you and complain about one another."

"Ouch! Okay, so what was I supposed to do differently?" Jack asked, defeat weighing every word. "I want to be a leader who supports my team and has an open-door policy. They all escalate their issues to me. I'm their boss. It's my job to listen and remove obstacles."

"Yes and no," Meg countered. "Yes, remove obstacles, but no, not as a go-between. Removing obstacles means encouraging them to try to work things out on their own. If that fails, then your team should have clear guidance from you that they can escalate problems to you together, not separately." She leaned toward the screen. "With Brett and Shauna, even with the three of you in the same room, you should not play referee. You've got to be a neutral facilitator who makes sure everyone stays productive and respectful during the conversation. This is how strong teams learn to build good working relationships—through mutual trust and respect, which has to be modeled by you as their CEO."

"C'mon, Meg," Jack said, tilting his head back. "That all sounds great in theory, but name one team that works that way."

"You'd be surprised. When leaders set clear expectations and hold their people accountable, teams operate as they should—less drama and better performance. But it only works when leaders are disciplined and intentional about setting clear expectations and boundaries. What expectations and boundaries have you set for your team about how you want them to engage with one another?"

Jack ran his finger across the etched, narrow edge of the desk slowly and said softly, "I didn't think I'd have to hold everyone's hands like this. I just expected them to behave like adults."

"I get it. But it's not hand-holding I'm talking about; it's clear, specific communication of your expectations. People can't read your mind. You have to tell them—Shauna, Hannah, Brett, Don, Rob, everyone."

Jack stood up and picked up the soccer ball next to his desk, making sure he was still visible to Meg on the computer screen. He started bouncing the ball on his knees. "Sorry. It helps me think."

Meg grinned. "Have at it!"

"So, let's say I set these expectations about how everyone should engage with one another and with me." Jack's eyes stayed focused on the ball to ensure it stayed in the air as he bounced it from knee to knee. "This only solves the interaction problem. What about the problem of everyone missing the bigger picture and their role in making the one-year picture a reality?"

"Well, actually . . ." Meg started slowly.

"Hang on!" Jack caught the ball in his hands and slumped back into his chair. "It's the same thing, right? I have to be clear about how I expect each of them to help the team achieve these goals and what mindset shift I need to see from each of them."

"Yes!" Meg clapped her hands together. "You then reinforce your expectations by giving individuals positive feedback when they get things right and constructive feedback when they miss the mark. That's how you hold them accountable."

Jack nodded and stared out the window as a flash of lightning and a resounding clap of thunder tore through the steady sound of the rainstorm outside.

"Okay, I think I owe everyone more clarity around all my expectations," Jack said, slowly turning back toward the screen. "I really can't say I've spent much time on accountability, so I can make these changes. On the other hand, I think I've been abundantly clear with Brett about what I've needed from him. I've given him the feedback over and over and spent a ton of time with him, even as I'm essentially doing his job. But he's made no progress."

"Yes, and you've already had an honest conversation with him that you're considering other options." Meg took a sip of her tea. "So, what's your next step?"

"I'm still not sure." Jack slowly shook his head. "For years, this guy was so loyal to me when I was the Chief Revenue Officer. I'd just point him in a direction, and he'd go execute and get things done. But now it's like he has no clue where to start and gets angry when anyone tries to help."

"True, but to be fair, he is in a totally different role now. When you were CRO, you set a strategy and created a framework in which your team could operate effectively. As a result, he was able to thrive. Now, you're asking him to come up with his own strategy and framework so his sales team can penetrate strategic accounts. It could be that this isn't his skill set."

"Okay, but then why does he get so defensive even after I've talked to him about it? Why not just let us all help him?"

Meg smiled, looking Jack right in the eye. "Jack, what was your reaction to Renata's suggestion that you needed an executive coach?"

"Well, I . . ." Jack shook his head. "Shit! You're right."

She laughed, then said, "We've covered a lot today. But you need to think hard about Brett. He takes up a lot of your time and energy—and you've said it yourself, he's not making progress. You can't keep going like this." She smiled to soften her words. "You're under tremendous pressure from the board. I know he's been this great, loyal lieutenant to you over the years, but push that aside and ask yourself if Brett is the one to empower Accelx to achieve your one-year vision and beyond."

"Yeah," Jack said in a defeated tone. "I need to think about whether it's time to face the music with Brett. Thanks, Meg. Talk soon."

CHAPTER 14

APRIL 15
10:07 A.M.

"AND SO, THIS is the kind of team I want us to have at Accelx. A team that respects one another, that works together seamlessly to advance the company's goals. Imagine what it would be like to work in a positive environment where we're not left second-guessing every interaction. There would be no meetings after the meeting, no more single escalations behind people's backs, but rather a unified team focused on our customers and our employees and doing right by them. That's what I know this team can do, and it's the only way we can lead Accelx to success. Do you guys have any questions?"

Jack was standing at the head of the conference room table over a week later scanning his leadership team, who were situated around the maple table. He had used the last week and a half to organize his thoughts and have individual conversations about his expectations. Now, he was addressing them as a team. He chose to stand rather than sit, to emphasize his zero tolerance policy.

He attempted to get a silent acceptance by making eye contact with each member of the team. Their sheepish reaction reminded Jack of the look on Jamie's and Quinn's faces when he'd admonished them for asking him to mediate a fight over a toy two nights ago. He felt more like a dad than ever. He quickly pushed that thought aside, remembering the importance of clarity that he and Meg had discussed. After a few moments, he sat to get down to business.

"With that out of the way," he said. "Let's get to our agenda. How's it going with the new lead gen company, Brett? Any ideas as to when we'll be able to make the switch?"

"We'll be up and running by the end of this week," Brett started. "I can already see the difference this is going to make to our pipeline. Don and I gave notice to our old provider yesterday."

Jack nodded. "Thanks again to Shauna and Don for deferring their two new hires by a quarter to fund the additional cost. If it all works as planned, we should be in a position to hire those folks by August."

"Well, we didn't really have a choice," Don snapped, but then he noticed Jack's admonishing expression. "Sorry, everyone. What I meant to say is that me and my team are committed to the goals we all discussed a few weeks ago. You told me to focus on company over function, and I heard you loud and clear."

"Well, I appreciate you guys taking one for the team." Brett smiled at Don and Shauna and then turned to face Jack. "I don't mean to cut and run here, but I am totally swamped with the implementation and would like to get back to the team as soon as possible. Is there anything else you need from me in this meeting, boss? I will send you the sales activity report and send an update on the pipeline to the entire team."

"That'll do," Jack acknowledged. "Thanks, Brett. Oh, and I put in a call to the CEO of Mediks. I will let you know what I hear back."

"I didn't know you were going to call the CEO," Brett said. "I thought Josie was managing that account?"

Jack tried to hide his frustration. "I got a note from Josie asking if I could help her because they went silent. You were copied."

"Right!" Brett pointed his index finger at Jack. "Sorry, I've been totally consumed by the lead gen implementation. Yes, please do keep me posted."

Jack watched Brett gather his things and walk out the door. He tried to keep his face neutral given the discussion he had just had with his team, but he could feel his blood boiling. He took a breath and turned to Hannah.

"Hannah, what's the latest on the Onergize implementation?"

"Incremental progress but still progress—so that's good. I've got a meeting with our customer lead tomorrow." Hannah opened her tablet and scrolled down. She turned to Rob. "Rob, did you have a chance to review the list of software enhancements I sent?"

A look of annoyance flashed across Rob's face until he made eye contact with Jack and quickly neutralized his expression. Jack reminded himself to be patient with the team and that this was going to take time.

"Not yet." Rob cleared his throat. "I'll get to it before the end of the day. But again, I don't think these are technology challenges."

Jack sat back in his chair. They'd been stuck making only incremental progress for some time. They needed to try something new. He stood up and walked over to the south-facing picture windows in the conference room and peered down at the park across the street. It was spring break, and the playground was full of kids. They looked like tiny little specs from the thirty-seventh floor, but Jack could make out that they were swinging, sliding, and running around on the large, padded playground. *They look so free and uninhibited*, he thought. *Maybe that's our problem . . . we're thinking about this problem within our current perspective. Maybe we need to open our minds and think more broadly about this issue.* That train of thought inspired an idea.

"Team," he said, turning from the window to face them, "we've been stuck making incremental progress with Onergize for too long. We need a big push to get this relationship back on the right track. Maybe we could try evaluating this problem from different perspectives. Indulge me for a moment?"

The team looked intrigued, so he continued. "Hannah, can you please describe to me how you think Rob views our challenges with the Onergize implementation?"

Hannah looked confused. "I'm not sure I follow. You want me to explain Rob to you?"

"Kind of, yes." Jack walked back to the table and sat down at the head of it. "I want you to explain to me how you think Rob views the core problem with the Onergize implementation."

"Honestly?" Hannah sat in silence for a few moments, seeming to process Jack's question. "Well, I think he believes that his technology is flawless and that these software issues and enhancements we're raising are all customer or ops user errors."

"What?" Rob said, incredulous. "That's ridiculous. I've never said anything like that. No technology is flawless. You know we have over one hundred recorded bugs in our system that we're systematically working through—plus all the enhancements we need to continue servicing our customers."

"Well, you don't act like it!" Hannah retorted. "You're always arguing with me about any issue I raise."

Rob shook his head. "Hannah, it's my job to distinguish between a training issue, enhancement, bug, or anything else so I can make sure this technology is robust for every Accelx customer. You mistake my comments as arguments when they are really a fact-finding effort."

Jack turned to Rob. "Okay, Rob, it's your turn. Explain to me how Hannah views the core problem with the Onergize implementation."

"That's easy," Rob opined. "In Hannah's world, the customer is always right and Accelx is always to blame. The problem is always either the way we sold the software or the tech supporting it. Her team is always caught in the middle."

"No way!" Hannah argued. "We're always pushing back on customer leads who have ridiculous demands. Maybe you just don't see it. Our sales team does a great job of setting expectations with our existing channels, and our tech is superb, perhaps the best in the market!"

"Wait . . ." Rob pulled his head back in shock. "You think our tech is superb?"

"Of course I do," Hannah responded, with a hint of annoyance. "This tech makes our team so efficient and, for the most part, makes the customer's life so easy."

A loud crack filled the room as the air-conditioning kicked on. In a few seconds, it dulled into a faint noise of air blowing through the vents. While the room cooled down, Jack was processing this exchange and contemplating whether the next move was his or someone else's in the room.

"You guys both seem to be taking a set of basic facts and spinning your own narratives around it," Shauna observed. A few others at the table began to nod. "It's getting in the way of your progress. Maybe the two of you—actually, maybe all of us—need to start assuming good intent and being curious instead of making assumptions and judgments."

"That sounds like a great place to start," Jack added, seeing nodding heads around the conference room.

Rob leaned forward in his chair and straightened his polo shirt. "Hannah, I value your input from the field. I need it to make sure our product does its job for our customers. I very much see you as my partner in this. I'm sorry if I've given you any other impression."

"I appreciate that, Rob." Hannah smiled. "So why do you think these aren't tech issues that need to be fixed to stabilize Onergize?"

Rob exhaled loudly. "The problems they've described thus far feel more like they're not using the software as designed. But maybe I'm missing something. I'm happy to take another look with a more open mind."

"Maybe we should sit together and go through it?" Hannah suggested. "Two heads are better than one, right? Maybe we've both lost sight of that recently."

Rob smiled back, but before he could respond, the door to the conference room swung open and Jack's assistant pushed into the room.

"Sorry to interrupt." Dean scanned the room, trying to locate his boss. "Jack, I have the CEO from Mediks on the phone. You said I should come get you if he called."

"I'll be right there." Turning back to his leadership team, he said, "I'll catch you guys later. Shauna, can you take over for me?" Then Jack stood up and raced back to his office.

CHAPTER 15

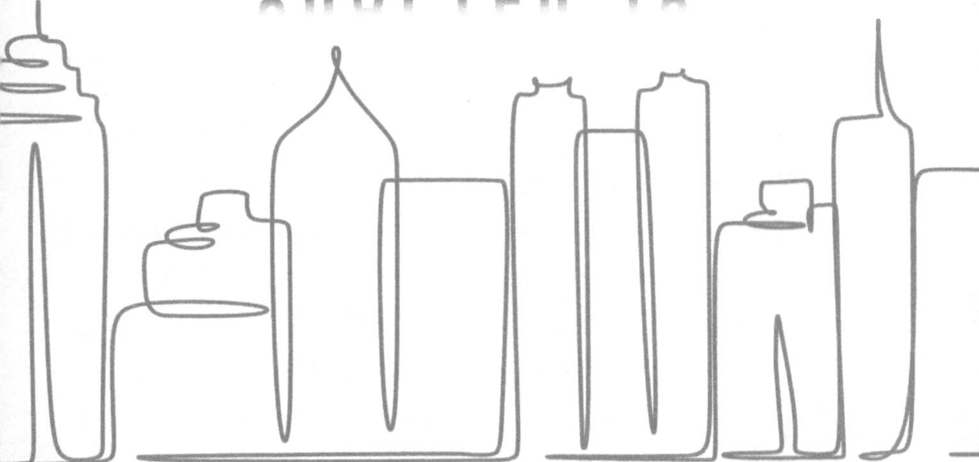

"THE RELEASE IS on-target for next week," Rob said, handing Jack a summary report. "It'll make my team a bit more efficient. It permanently fixes all the code we had to work around for Onergize. It should help Onergize stabilize further too."

"That's fantastic!" Jack scanned the document for a moment and then returned his gaze to his CTO. "So, is this an admission that there were technology issues?" Jack smiled. "This isn't about blame, but I think it offers a learning opportunity."

"Yeah, sorry about that." Rob looked sheepish. "I apologized to Hannah too and bought her lunch last week. We've agreed to continue operating as partners. I'm not sure how we lost our way on that, but it won't happen again."

"Great to hear." Jack smiled. "One follow-up question: How much of the coding fix was your effort versus your team's?"

Rob looked down at the vinyl plank floor and was silent. They were seated at the conference table in Jack's office, eight days after he had laid down his behavior expectations to the entire team, for their weekly one-on-one meeting. It was almost a quarter after nine, but Jack could already feel the early summer heat rising from his office window. They were in for a scorcher today, and he was grateful he could enjoy the comfort of his air-conditioned office all day long.

"Okay, let me ask the question differently," Jack said, breaking the awkward silence. "Did your team contribute to this effort at all, or did you pull an all-nighter to make code changes?"

"No all-nighters. I haven't done that since Marcie had colic," Rob said, chuckling. "But I definitely contributed."

"Like twenty-five percent?" Jack inquired.

"We both know where this is going." Rob shook his head. "I get the board's feedback that I need to be a better leader, but this was an emergency. My team is totally spent trying to keep the workarounds in place for Onergize, so I had to jump in and help make the code changes."

"I would accept that response if this were the exception. But you know well and good that with you, this heavy involvement is the rule. We can't keep going on like this. Your team's engagement numbers are among the lowest across the company. Even before the board's feedback, Shauna and I were coaching you on how to lead your team." Jack sat back and tried to make eye contact with his CTO. "But we're not seeing improvement. Please help me understand. We want to help you. What are we missing?"

Rob sat quietly. It took everything Jack had to stop talking and lean into the silence, but he wanted to give Rob the time he needed to gather his thoughts and reflect on the statements he'd made.

Jack watched Rob gently nod his head before looking up with a defeated expression. "Honestly? I get the technical stuff. It's like I can see the problem and solution so clearly. It comes so naturally. It's always been that way for me. But the people side is so hard. My instincts are always wrong."

"Well, I'm not sure any of us are naturally great at the people stuff. No one ever has it one-hundred percent figured out. We just have to keep learning and trying." Jack smiled. "Look at the discussion I had with the team last week about expectations. I didn't know to do that, I had to learn that I was responsible for what was happening with our team dynamic because I wasn't clear about my expectations. But, let me ask you, were you always a technical genius? Would you have been able to architect Accelx's servicing platform right after college?"

"Of course not!" Rob exclaimed. "I mean, I was good, but nobody's *that* good. It's cutting edge! You know it got Accelx where it is. And I—"

"Let me stop you there." Jack raised his right hand. "I'm not disagreeing, but I want to focus on our discussion. We all have to work on ourselves to strengthen our talents, refine our skills, and address our weaknesses. You are the CTO now, not a programmer or a technical architect. Given your role, my expectation is that you work at developing your leadership skills and lead your team. You don't get a pass because you're a technical genius. Am I clear?"

"Yes. I get it." Rob looked down at the vinyl plank floor again.

"Look, don't be so hard on yourself," Jack said gently. "I've known you for years and I've seen your people instincts in action—and honestly, they're pretty good. I see it in the way you talk about your kids and your family. And remember, a few years ago, when Lisa's son was diagnosed with the heart condition?"

Rob nodded but didn't look up.

"You were so supportive of her and her family, helping her figure out the leave process, keeping in touch with her throughout, and rallying the company behind her family. She wrote us such a beautiful note when she returned to work—and that was in large part due to your role."

"Anyone would have done that," Rob argued halfheartedly. "She had a kid with a life-threatening disease."

"Not at the level you did," Jack countered. "You have it inside of you. You just have to trust yourself and keep strengthening that muscle. Have you been meeting with Shauna regularly like we discussed?"

"No, sorry, I've been too busy." Rob sighed. "I'll get those back on the calendar."

"Good," Jack said. "No more excuses. This must be your top priority. I want to see a positive improvement in your engagement numbers during our next pulse survey, which is in ninety days."

"That's a lot to ask, boss!" Rob exclaimed. "I'm not sure I can turn this around in such a short time."

"Well, I suggest you get with Shauna right away to figure that out," Jack replied. "This is the only way you will take this seriously, and I know if you put your mind to it the way you put your mind to a technical challenge, you can get there."

"What about Onergize and all of those other implementations?" Rob asked, eyes wide. "I still have a ton of work to do. I need to spend time on the technical stuff too. Who is going to do all this stuff? I mean, we can't meet our board mandate if I'm not focused on the right things, and then what—"

"Rob," Jack interjected in a firm tone. "Do you hear how many times you said 'I' in that reply? The only way we, as a company, can be successful meeting our mandate is if you lead your team and position it for success. With the number of currently scheduled implementations and the increasing growth of future implementations, you're going to get overwhelmed. You have to train and delegate, or else we won't be able to scale effectively, especially in new verticals. We've got to fix this—fast!"

Rob looked shocked and remained quiet for a few moments. "Did you have anything else you wanted to discuss today?" he uttered in a quiet voice.

"Hey, don't be discouraged. I know you can do this. Let me know if I can help in any way." Jack stood up. "That's it for now. I'll see you at our Onergize meeting later this afternoon."

Rob nodded, gathered his things, and shuffled out of Jack's office. Jack returned to his desk.

I'm such a hypocrite. I'm telling Rob that he's got to stop doing his team's work when I'm still doing Brett's job. The Mediks thing was a disaster. Thank God I was able to right the ship and get them signed.

Jack slumped in his chair and exhaled, trying to calm himself down. A few moments later, he heard a gentle knock on his door.

"Jack?" Don asked. "I wanted to let you know that Onergize's second invoice payment came in. Looks like we may be out of immediate danger for now."

"That's great." Jack managed a weak smile. "Thanks for letting me know."

"You okay, boss?" Don looked concerned.

"Yeah, sorry." Jack sat up in his chair. "Just a bit tired."

"Got it." Don hovered in the doorway. "It's been thirty days since the board gave us the directive, and we're at least making good progress on our financial targets. I just sent you the latest report. Revenue from strategic accounts is definitely looking better, thanks to the recent ones in pharma and medical devices, but I think you knew that already."

"I had a pretty good idea," Jack said, winking. "But thanks for confirming."

Don took a step into Jack's office. "Hey, I know you're planning to bring in lunch for today's leadership team meeting about the Onergize implementation. Why don't we bring in food from LaRue?"

"LaRue for an internal meeting?" Jack asked, taken aback. "What about your very public stance that we only bring in LaRue for external meetings?"

"I'm bending the rules a bit!" Don chuckled. "Things are starting to look up. We've been working hard, and it's nice to have a treat. Plus, Hannah and I had a tough but fair conversation the other day after you talked to us, and I realized that sometimes my behavior could mistakenly lead people to believe I'm the cheapskate of the thirty-seventh floor."

"I think that comes with the territory, doesn't it?" Jack laughed.

Don smiled. "Well, I want us to be smart about our money, but I don't want to cripple the business. Hannah had some good examples of where my team and I may be overly focused on the numbers to the detriment of the business."

"I'm glad you guys had a good discussion. Like we've talked about, you and your team play a key role in enabling our growth." Jack smiled. "And you're right, things are looking up, but we still have plenty of work to do. Today's meeting will be challenging, as I'm planning to ask the team some tough questions to ensure Onergize goes from being out of immediate danger to fully satisfied, as well as to ensure future implementations are seamless. LaRue will be a nice counterbalance to that. Thanks for thinking of it."

"See you in a bit." Don turned around and left Jack's office.

Jack opened his email and scrolled to Don's financial report. *Don's right. Revenue is up across all segments. We've made decent progress on strategic accounts, and profitability is on-target. This is all positive.*

He leaned back in his chair and interlaced his fingers behind his head. *I wonder if I got through to Rob? This was the least defensive I've seen him, so that's hopeful. We still have to work on his ego, but that's for another day.*

Jack got up, turned around, and stared out his window. He did a few leg lifts and butt kicks to get his circulation going after sitting for so long.

But the board's going to be all over me about Brett. I can't keep driving all the strategic sales. Jack covered his face with his hands. *If Brett can't even close one strategic sale himself, how does he expect his team to meet the challenge? He just can't seem to get there as a leader. Maybe it's time for a change.*

"Shit. This sucks," he mumbled out loud. He tried to rub the tension out of his neck as he picked up the phone and dialed.

"Hi Renata. It's Jack. Do you have a minute? I want to talk to you about your Gold database of sales leaders."

CHAPTER 16

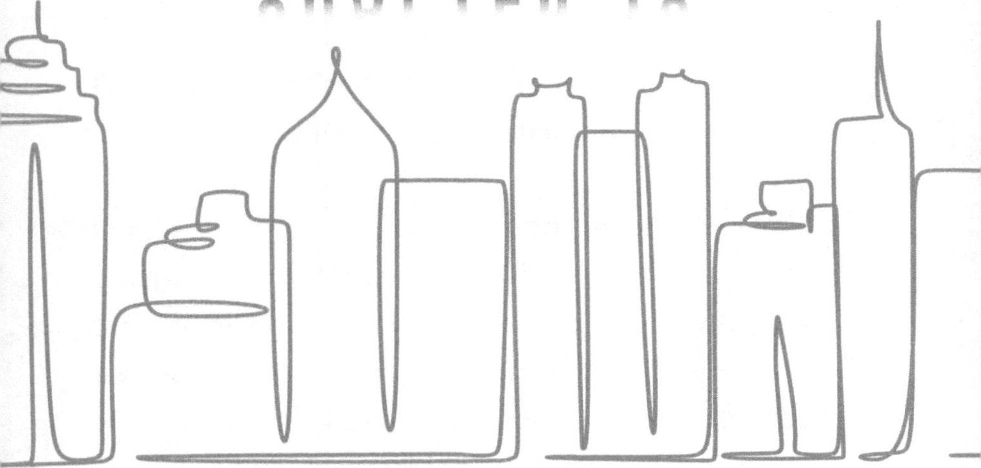

MAY 5
5:08 P.M.

"GOOD THING I changed into jeans," Jack said to Shauna as he gently kicked sawdust with his leather dress sneaker two weeks later. He glanced around at the huge TVs tuned in to soccer, tennis, and baseball games while he waited for the bartender to pour his beer from the tap. It was a few minutes after five in Southern California, and it had been a long day. Hours of early morning phone calls with East Coast clients and team members had turned into many more hours of West Coast meetings. Exhausted, Jack glanced at the time on his phone. "Meg strikes me as a sort of, I don't know, formal person, right? I'm kind of surprised she chose this place."

"Well, based on her description, I told her that I thought you'd like it." Shauna smiled and scanned the room. "Meg is way more of a jeans-and-beer kind of person than you give her credit for—and I know you are too."

"Cheers!" Jack lifted his freshly poured schooner of beer and took a sip, then he handed the bartender his credit card. "Keep the tab open."

"C'mon, let's head out to the patio. We've got a few minutes before Meg gets here, and it's such a nice day." Shauna put on her sunglasses, picked up her schooner, and charted a path through the long communal tables with picnic-style benches. Jack followed, taking in the aroma of grilling burgers and frying onions, which suddenly made him very hungry.

They made their way to a rectangular patio and found a table with an umbrella. For a Wednesday evening, the patio had a decent crowd. Shauna placed her beer down on the table and headed to a cylindrical oak barrel in the middle of the patio. She threw back the plastic hatch, grabbed a bowl from the stack next to the barrel, and scooped out peanuts. She made her way back to the table. Jack texted Meg and told her they were out on the patio and to use his tab when she arrived.

"Peanuts?" Shauna plopped the bowl down in the middle of the table. "You're supposed to throw the shells on the floor. Enjoy!"

"Very cool." Jack lifted his schooner and looked around at the peanut-shell covered patio. "This is a solid pour, at a decent price too! Thanks for your help today, Shauna. I'm excited to meet Meg in person."

"Cheers!" Shauna tapped her glass with Jack's. "Dang, this is a bicep workout!"

Jack laughed. Then he grabbed a handful of peanuts from the bowl, shelled them, and popped them in his mouth. He eased back in his chair as he dropped a fistful of shells on the concrete.

"Good to hear you laugh." Shauna smiled. "It's been a while."

"Yeah." Jack brushed away peanut dust from his jeans. "I have to say, things finally feel like they're turning around. I know there's still plenty of work to do, but Onergize seems like it's on a better path now. It took effort, but getting Hannah and Rob to stop working against each other has gone a long way."

"You did a good job getting people to focus on the core problem with that exercise where we looked at things from different perspectives," Shauna said as she adjusted her sunglasses.

"I have to say, the team responded well. It helped us design a great process to keep Onergize on a good path and for future implementations."

They both sat quietly, soaking in the beautiful Southern California sun, sipping beer, shelling peanuts, and throwing the broken shells on the floor. Unusually, it had rained the day before, clearing the air and making way for a spectacular view of the San Gabriel Mountains from their table.

"Jack," Shauna started slowly, "I also wanted to thank you for bringing me into your confidence and asking me to join you on this trip. I appreciated your honest feedback with the team. I realize that my behavior with Brett was part of the problem.

I know better now, and I'm genuinely sorry for not being more professional. It won't happen again."

Jack nodded and took a long sip of beer. While he felt good about the actions he was taking to get Accelx back on track, the past few weeks had definitely been the most hectic he'd experienced since taking over as CEO. After discussing his concerns about Brett with Renata, she'd put him in touch with a handful of potential sales leaders who had worked with Gold portfolio companies before. Three of them lived in Southern California, and since he also had a few strong strategic account prospects in the area, he decided to make the trip out. He asked Shauna to join him for part of the trip to evaluate the candidates to replace Brett.

"I appreciate it." Jack tried to meet his colleague's eyes. "I know I also played a part in our team's dynamic, and I'm also committed to doing better. But, like we discussed, as the people leader, it's your job to set the example, and that's what I'm going to hold you to going forward."

"I understand," Shauna replied. "Like I said, I'm embarrassed you had to call me out about my behavior in the first place. I know better, but it was an important wake-up call for me."

"I know you do," Jack said, smiling. "Don't beat yourself up. We all need to take responsibility here. I'm just as much to blame. But let's make a deal, okay? You and I will never sink to the lowest common denominator on any team again. Instead, we'll work hard to rise above and hold everyone—including ourselves—accountable for their behavior. Let's vow to model what it looks like to operate at the highest level. Deal?"

"Deal!" Shauna raised her glass.

"Hi you two!" Meg planted her schooner on the table and rested her sunglasses on the top of her head. "Thanks for the beer, Jack. Much appreciated."

"Meg!" Shauna stood up and embraced Meg in a tight hug. "It's so good to see you."

"Likewise, my girl!" Meg turned to Jack and extended her hand. "And, Jack, it's great to finally meet you in person."

"It's wonderful to finally meet you in person too." Jack took her hand in both of his, squeezed it appreciatively, and smiled. "You're exactly what I pictured, albeit a little shorter."

Meg laughed. "Yeah, everyone thinks I'm much taller over video, but I'm only 5'4" on a good day."

"Have a seat," Jack said, releasing Meg's hand and pointing to the empty chair. "How far do you live from here?"

"Just a few miles," Meg replied, scooching her chair toward the table. "But I took a rideshare so I could imbibe with you guys." She gave a mischievous smile and took a sip of her cold beer.

"We did too," Shauna replied, lifting her schooner. "It has been a *long* day. The last thing we wanted to do was navigate LA traffic. Driving out here is even worse than Atlanta!"

Jack held up his glass. "To you two. I'm so glad we could make this work."

The three of them clinked glasses. Meg was different than what Jack had expected, but in a good way. She seemed less buttoned-up and intense, more human in her dark blue jeans, casual white blouse, and gray sneakers. Watching her sip casually from a big schooner of beer made him smile.

Meg turned to face Shauna. "How's Sunil? Michelle mentioned she had a chance to spend time with you and him last week during a business trip."

"He's doing okay." Shauna tried a faint smile. "The treatments are rough. Some days are better than others. It was nice to see Michelle. I was telling Jack a few weeks ago that the entire Dominal crew has made excuses to get down to Atlanta over the last few months. They're so sweet."

"It's a solid group of people." Meg smiled. "They are probably some of the most genuine people I've ever met."

"For sure." Shauna fought back a tear.

"So, Jack," Meg said, motioning toward all the peanut shells on the floor. "What do you think of this place?"

"I love it!" Jack laughed. "But I'm surprised it's your cup of tea . . . or should I say beer?"

"Ha! There are a ton of swanky bars in SoCal with overpriced drinks," Meg said after taking a sip of her beer. "They may have great locations, but most of them lack character. There's an authentic vibe here—almost like SoCal's version of Cheers in Boston. You know, where everybody knows your name," she sang. "And the burgers aren't half bad either."

"You're right, it's Cheers with peanut shells and minus the snow." Jack laughed. "I'm all in. Can't wait to try the burgers."

"Trust me, you won't be disappointed!" Meg grabbed a handful of peanuts. "Let's get business out of the way so we can relax. How's the trip going so far?"

"Good!" Jack said. "I've had several solid meetings with potential customers, and at least one looks very promising.

Shauna flew in yesterday afternoon, and we had dinner with one of the sales candidates. We met the other two today, and now we're here. We've packed it in."

"Good for you," Meg responded as she shelled a few peanuts. "How were the sales leadership candidates?"

Jack and Shauna exchanged glances, and both grabbed their schooners for a sip of beer. It was obvious neither wanted to weigh in first.

"It can't be that bad," Meg chuckled. "Jack?"

"They were all super impressive," Jack replied, finally breaking the silence. "But I just don't know. This is a hard one for me. I think I know what I don't want, but I'm still figuring out what I do want."

"Okay." Meg turned to Shauna. "What about you?"

"Each of them had their strengths," Shauna answered, playing with a cardboard beer coaster imprinted with "Rose Mountain Bar and Grill" above a snowcapped mountain. "But I wouldn't jump to hire any of them just because Renata said they had success at a Gold portfolio company. I think we need to be smart here and open the search to an executive recruiter who can scan the market. Shotgun hires rarely work."

"I'm just worried about the time this is going to take," Jack weighed in. "We're on a short leash with the board, so we need to take action quickly here."

"You're right," Meg acknowledged. "We need to discuss this more, but first I could use some reinforcements. Burgers? More drinks?"

The three of them made their way back to the bar and picked up burgers, fries, and fresh beers. Heading back to the patio, Meg gave Shauna and Jack a quick geography lesson so they could better understand where they were in Southern California.

"We're just east of Pasadena, but what's awesome about this place is the Rose Parade floats make their way down this very street on New Year's Eve before they line up for the parade," Meg explained. "You can sit here, enjoy a beer, and watch the floats be towed into position."

"That's so cool!" Shauna exclaimed. "I watch the Rose Parade every year. It's on my bucket list to see it in person."

"Let me know when you want to come," Meg said as she unwrapped her burger. "It's way better to get tickets to the stands as opposed to camping all night."

"Definitely!" Shauna's excitement was palpable.

"Oh man," Jack muttered, his mouth full of food, "these burgers do not disappoint. I'm going to have to find more reasons to come to SoCal."

"I told you!" Meg laughed.

They wolfed down their burgers and fries as the sun started to dip behind the mountains. The conversation flowed naturally. The pink sunset backlit the mountains, and Jack found himself mesmerized by the colors and the view.

"I could get used to this." Jack sighed, easing back in his chair, feeling relaxed and satiated. "The food, the view, the peanut shells . . . I get why you like this place, Meg." Jack gave her a playful smile.

"Yeah," Meg laughed, "it's one of my favorites—but not somewhere I'd take *every* client. Some prefer the overpriced drinks and trendy vibe."

"Nah, this is perfect," Shauna said before taking a sip of her dwindling beer.

"So, tell me more about the sales leaders you met." Meg leaned forward in her chair. "Did any of them have experience penetrating new markets? Did any have a background in pharma or medical devices?"

"Each had bits and pieces," Jack replied, playing with his half-empty beer mug. "For example, Scott Masters has grown an existing presence in pharma and likely has good contacts in the space, but he's never penetrated a new market, so that's a concern."

"Yeah, and Bryan Chung has penetrated new markets but is a medical devices and pharma novice," Shauna added. "He was also arrogant. I don't think he'd be a good addition to our team."

"Agreed," Jack weighed in. "I think he could help us get on track over the next six months, but in the long term, I don't think he's the type of guy who could lead a sales team to success. We'd be constantly cleaning up after him."

"Okay, got it. This is all very useful." Meg took off her sunglasses as the sun faded completely behind the mountains. "And what about the third candidate?"

"Maria Humphries was interesting," Shauna offered. "I actually think she would align well with our culture. But I'm not confident she could turn things around quickly."

"Agreed. She has the right experience for the long-term CRO we need," Jack said, nodding. "If it were eighteen months ago, maybe she could have worked. But with our backs against the wall, I don't know if she's going to roll up her sleeves and get it done for us in the short term."

"But she has had success at a Gold company before, right?" Meg looked down, folding her napkin. "I mean, Gold is the real deal. You gotta be pretty agile to get a recommendation from Renata."

"Agreed," Shauna chimed in. "But you know the drill. Some people are really good at organizing chaos—they know how to stop the bleeding. I'm not sure she has that skill set, but it's something we desperately need."

"Ah, I see what you're saying. So, Maria is more like the specialist who comes in after the patient has been stabilized and takes it from there."

"Yeah. Renata likes her a lot," Jack added. "But she's also only worked at one Gold company. And it sounds like the situation and environment were completely different. Like I said, I need to give it more thought."

"The types of people who thrive in investor-backed companies are those who can fix the wing while still flying the plane," Meg observed. "I'd share your feedback with Renata and get her thoughts. She suggested each of these candidates for a reason. Maybe it was just to open your eyes to what's out there. But you can't dwell on this too long. Perhaps you should consider it as two different problems. Figure out how to stabilize and get the team to hit your short-term goal, then figure out how to set up your team for long-term success. In the short-term, you might need two people to get the job done."

Shauna nodded. "I was starting to go down that path. Maybe we don't need just one person. We need to get you some immediate relief, Jack. You're juggling way too much right now."

"Two people? That just makes things infinitely harder for us, right?" Jack finished the rest of his beer. "Lots to consider."

Meg nodded. "Well, let's move on to something more fun. When was the last time you were in California?" The tone of the conversation then shifted to something more light-hearted, and they spent the next hour regaling each other with war stories from the corporate world. After another round of beers and too many laughs, Jack checked his watch. "We really should be going—early flight tomorrow."

Meg and Shauna nodded, and the three of them made their way to the bar. Jack took care of the bill, and they all headed out to the parking lot to wait for their cars to arrive.

"Jack, thanks again for dinner," Meg said. "It was so great to spend time with the two of you."

"My pleasure, Meg! We're still on for our Friday call, right? I'll be back in Atlanta by then, and I'll likely need your help to figure out this sales leader position. Shauna and I will work out timing and talking points for Brett on the flight home tomorrow."

"You bet!" Meg turned to Shauna. "Always amazing to see you. I'm so impressed by all you've accomplished. Keep knocking it out of the park!"

"Thanks, Meg. Great to see you too." Shauna smiled and leaned in for a hug.

Meg waved as she jumped into her rideshare. A few moments later, it was Jack and Shauna's turn to get into their car. Once en route, Jack pulled out his phone and started to scroll through his emails. He saw one from Mahesh Patil, the CEO of ThriVn, one of Accelx's signature customers in the long-term care space. It was marked urgent.

Jack,

We need to connect tomorrow. My team has been escalating issues to Accelx for the past three months and nothing is getting resolved. It seems to be getting worse. Given our long-standing relationship, I wanted to give you a chance to address the issues. But let me be clear, we are seriously reconsidering whether to continue our partnership with Accelx. Please advise on some times that work for you.

Mahesh

CHAPTER 17

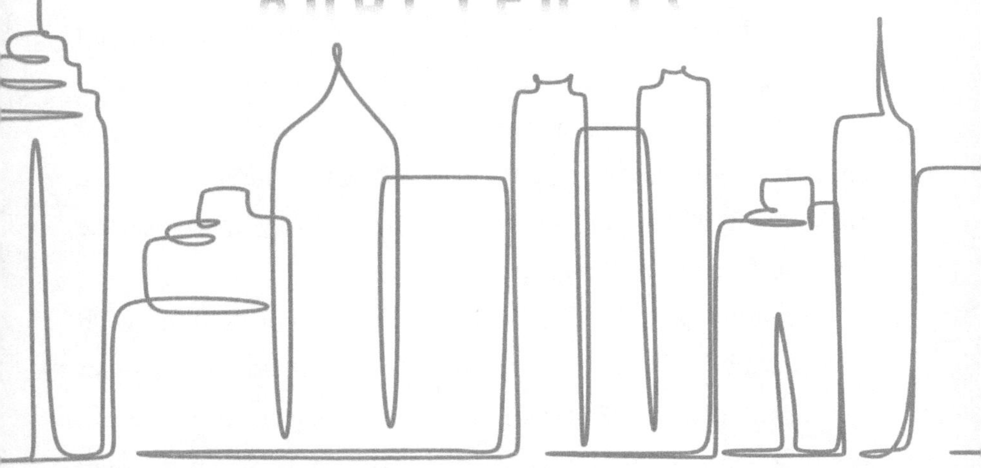

TWO DAYS LATER, Jack pushed open the double doors to the conference room. It was his first day back after his trip to California. He'd been in the office since seven and was feeling the need for more caffeine, which would have to wait for now.

On his way back from Los Angeles, he'd made a pit stop in Chicago to meet with Mahesh in person to delve into ThriVn's service challenges. Hannah had flown out and met him there, along with Accelx's account manager, Sabrina

Nguyen, who was still in Chicago to provide on-site support until the account was fully functional again.

Jack managed a tired smile as he sat at the head of the table and faced Don, Rob, and Hannah. "Hi everyone. Just a side note before we begin—Brett and Shauna won't be joining us. Look, I know it's been a hectic couple of days, and I appreciate all of you jumping in to help. Also, thank you for coming into the office today to meet in-person. I got a note from Mahesh just now thanking us for addressing their issues, but it didn't sound like we were out of the woods just yet. Hannah, can you provide the latest updates from the ground?"

Hannah straightened in her chair. "I checked in with Sabrina an hour ago and things are stabilized. Rob's team quickly identified the bug and put in a workaround. Sabrina is coming back tonight but is planning to go out there next week to make sure things continue to go smoothly."

"We'll have a permanent fix for the bug with the next release in two weeks," Rob added. "It's too risky to implement it before the team has fully tested everything. Jonas on my team is leading the effort. My team is also digging into what caused the bug in the first place. I have a feeling we may have inadvertently caused it with the system updates we've been doing to stabilize our strategic accounts. We're implementing a more robust testing program regardless."

Jack nodded and leaned back in his chair. He was dog-tired from traveling, the early-morning and late-night phone calls, the stress of this week, and his crazy morning, but he had to focus on the task at hand right now.

"Team," he said, "I think one thing that would be helpful is to figure out exactly how we got here. It's important for us to make sure we've structurally—not just technically—fixed this issue so it won't happen again."

"I take full responsibility," Hannah chimed in. "ThriVn was reporting issues, and those issues were being inputted into our ticketing system, but for some reason, they didn't get escalated properly. Also, because we've been all-hands-on-deck with the strategic accounts, no one on my team was looking at the tickets holistically to see the pattern and take action." She held up a hand. "It's not an excuse by any means, but at least we've identified the problem so we can improve the process. We're reworking our process to make sure it doesn't happen again, and I'll come back to this team if it really is a resource issue. Rob and I are meeting after this to figure out why our ticketing system didn't flag these issues properly."

"Actually, Hannah, after you called me last night, I asked my team to dig into the ticketing system, and it turns out we didn't load the latest patch, which fixed the bug with escalations," Rob volunteered. "So, this problem is on us too. No excuses, but we didn't get the service bulletin."

"Why didn't we get a service bulletin?" Jack asked. "We're a paying customer, right?"

Rob stayed quiet for a moment, exchanging glances with both Hannah and Don. He seemed to be gathering the courage to speak.

"Rob, it's okay," Jack said gently. "I'm not here to blame anyone. I just want to understand what's happening. What are the reasons why we don't receive service bulletins from IT vendors?"

"There are a few reasons," Rob started. "Sometimes they go to our junk folders, sometimes my team just misses them. Sometimes they get delayed if we are late to pay their bills. But we checked everywhere, and we didn't get the service bulletin."

"Okay." Jack nodded. "Don, what can you tell me about the payment?"

"Well," Don said in a sheepish tone, "before the last board meeting, we held all nonessential payables to improve our cash flow. It's possible the TicketNow payment was part of that hold."

Jack took a deep breath and closed his eyes. "How did I not know about this? We had plenty of cash, right?

"Yeah," Don acknowledged. "I was trying to make the finance metrics even better than they were. It's a leftover directive from your predecessor. I should have discussed it with you."

Jack nodded. "Yes, you should have. Let's stop that practice immediately unless we absolutely have to, and I want to know about it before there are any more payments held back."

"Understood," Don said. "And based on our discussion, I offered ThriVn's CFO a discount for the three months. Plus, I suggested we could hold pricing flat for another year. My team modeled it, and we'll still be able to meet our financial targets even with those discounts."

"Good thinking. How did Brenda respond?" Jack asked.

"She seemed open." Don rubbed his shiny, bald head. "I am hoping the fact that I proactively reached out will help us here."

"I'm curious as to how Brett responded to the flat pricing on the renewal?" Hannah asked. "Is he okay with it?"

Don glanced nervously at Jack, who nodded at him to indicate he would handle the question.

"Team," Jack started, taking a deep breath. "I also asked you to come in today because I wanted to let you know that as of this morning, Brett is no longer with Accelx. We offered him a generous severance package to help him during his transition period. We appreciate his contribution to the company and years of service. But the bottom line is he couldn't get the sales team to acquire strategic accounts, which is paramount to our strategy. I'll pause now and let you ask questions."

Rob and Hannah sat in stunned silence. Don fidgeted nervously. Jack scanned the room, trying to get a read. He fought the need to fill the silence with words, as he wanted everyone to process the news for a few moments.

"I worked with Brett for a very long time," Don said sadly, finally breaking the silence. "I'm going to miss him."

"Yeah, but I understand your decision, Jack," Hannah followed up. "You've been the one bringing in the strategic accounts. But I can't imagine what Accelx is going to be like without him."

Jack stared out the window of the conference room, trying to gather his thoughts before continuing.

"He will surely be missed. And our friendships with him don't have to end just because he's not here," Jack acknowledged with sadness in his voice. "I drafted a communication that we'll send to the entire company, and Shauna's putting together talking points for you and your direct reports to use with your teams. She and I are planning to meet with the sales team later this morning. Once this goes out, I expect all of you to meet with your teams to make sure this gets communicated properly and all questions get answered consistently."

"Are you going to run sales for now?" Hannah asked.

"Great question," Jack replied, turning to Hannah. "We're going to launch an external search for his replacement immediately, but in the interim, I'm bringing in an old business school colleague of mine who has extensive sales experience in a number of adjacent healthcare verticals that we've been focused on, including pharma and medical devices. His name is Steve Kimura. He's done work with Gold before and can penetrate strategic accounts while providing guidance to our team until we find a new leader."

"He doesn't want the job?" Rob asked.

"He's off the market." Jack smiled. "He made his money with some PE exits, and now he just does consulting. The board is fully supportive."

The team sat in silence again, and Jack let it linger for a minute before continuing. "Team, I just want to say how amazing it was that each of you took accountability for ThriVn's challenges. That's how a well-oiled machine works, and I'm glad to see we're getting there. But I am also accountable for what happened. When I was talking to Mahesh this week, I realized I've been so focused on acquiring strategic accounts that I haven't been paying attention to our existing customer base. I won't let that happen again, and I need each of you to hold me accountable."

They all nodded and sat quietly for another few moments.

"I know I'm throwing a lot at you today—especially on top of everything else we've been dealing with these last couple of weeks—but removing Brett from the sales leadership position simply couldn't wait any longer. It's going to be a hard day and a tough few weeks, but we will get through this," Jack continued. "Hannah, as our COO with the ultimate responsibility for customers, can you take the lead on making sure we track and fix all the structural issues that happened with ThriVn across all the functions? Let's continue to report on this during our weekly leadership meetings until we're completely sure everything is resolved."

"You got it, boss." Hannah saluted Jack, which made him smile.

"Thanks, guys." Jack stood up. "Let's reconvene one more time around two p.m. today to check in on everything. Based on that discussion, I will send an update to Mahesh."

"Jack?" Rob asked as the two of them exited the conference room. "Can we talk for a minute?"

"Sure." Jack gestured for Rob to follow him back to his office. They walked in silence down the hall. Once inside, Rob shut the door, and Jack took a seat at the conference table. "Have a seat. What's on your mind?"

"Well," Rob said, sitting down in the chair opposite Jack at the table, "I just wanted to ask how you're holding up. Today couldn't have been easy. You and Brett worked together for a very long time. I know he looked up to you like a father figure. I know you care a lot about him."

Jack fought back his emotions. He had been racing so fast the last few days, he hadn't paused to process that he was letting go of his friend and longtime colleague. Rob's questions brought it all the surface. He sat back in his chair, and his eyes started to moisten; he was too tired to hold it back.

"I'm not going to lie," he whispered, wiping away a few tears. "It has been one of the hardest weeks of my career. As leaders, we sometimes have to make the tough calls. I can only hope that Brett will keep an open mind and try to grow from this experience and that someday, we can all be friends again, having a beer in one of our backyards."

"Me too. Though I imagine it will be some time before he's ready to talk to any of us." Rob slumped back in his chair. "I know it's the right thing, but it's so hard. How do we reconcile these tough, uncomfortable, professional decisions with our sense of humanity?"

Jack pondered Rob's question for a bit. "Well, I think it's like any difficult thing in life—we don't get over it, but maybe over time we learn to live with the discomfort."

Rob nodded, and they both sat in silence for a few minutes. Jack found himself grateful for the momentary pause in a crazy day. Oddly enough, he felt comforted by Rob's presence.

"Jack," Rob said in a gentle tone, "if there's anything I can do to help you accept the discomfort, I hope you'll let me know."

"Thanks, Rob." Jack smiled warmly. "Just having you sit here with me and let me have a quiet moment to reflect amid the craziness has been huge. And this from a guy who says he doesn't have good people instincts," Jack said, chuckling.

"I never said I didn't care." Rob walked over and cupped Jack's right shoulder for a few seconds before he turned and made his way out of the office.

Jack sat at the table for another few minutes to process his conversation with Rob and the events of the day. It was now nearly eleven in the morning, and he was dying for a cup of coffee. He picked up his mug from his desk and made his way down the long hallway to the break room. Thankfully, the hallway was pretty empty. He needed some time to regroup.

"Hey, Jack!"

Startled, Jack had to find his balance again before turning around. "You scared me! I didn't think anyone was in the hallway. Must be lost in my own thoughts."

"So sorry." Shauna smiled apologetically. "I didn't mean to scare you. I just needed a cup of coffee. Quite a morning."

The two colleagues turned into the break room and headed for the coffee machine. Jack motioned for Shauna to pour her cup first.

"How's Brett?" Jack asked.

"He just left," Shauna said as she finished filling her cup. "He was pretty shaken up and wanted to be with his family. How did the team take it?"

"Okay, I think," Jack said, starting to fill his coffee mug. "They're going to miss him, but I think they understood. The timing stinks with everything we have going on, but like we talked about, there was never going to be a good time. Funny thing, though—Rob was super sweet. He came into my office afterward to make sure I was okay."

"He's a teddy bear with a hard shell." Shauna added some cream to her coffee, stirred, and inhaled the scent of her fresh coffee before taking a sip. "God, I love coffee," she said, sighing. "Rob has a lot of respect for you, particularly after you laid out your expectations. He told me no one's ever talked to him like that before, and he just didn't realize being the technical guru wasn't enough. He's committed to changing."

"That's good." Jack took a first sip of his coffee. "Did you see my communication about Brett?"

"Yeah, just read it. You did an excellent job communicating what the workforce needed to know instead of what you wanted to tell them. You're talking to them instead of at them. It'll go a long way. I sent the talking points for the leaders to you a few minutes ago, using the same style and key messages, so I think they will resonate." Shauna looked at her watch. "Ah, it's time to meet with the sales team. You ready?"

Jack took a deep breath and realized for the first time in a long time, he felt lighter, like a huge weight had been lifted. While he knew they weren't out of the woods with the board, strategic accounts, Onergize, or ThriVn, he finally felt confident that they were finally on the right track. For the first time since taking over as CEO, he felt like he was proactively running the company rather than reacting to the chaos around him.

He grinned at Shauna. "Yes, I'm ready. Let's go."

CHAPTER 18

"MR. SHORN, THEY'RE ready for you. Please follow me."

Jack stood up from the black faux-leather chair in the waiting room at Gold's headquarters and smoothed his gray polyester slacks. He followed the receptionist down a long walkway along a wall of picture windows framing the bright summer day in New York. He tried to slow his steps to take in the beautiful views of the city from each window, but the receptionist was moving too fast. After turning a corner, they arrived at a set of double doors made from bamboo with polished steel handles. The receptionist opened the door on the right and motioned for Jack to follow her into the room.

"Jack." Guillermo stood and walked toward him. He took Jack's hand in an extra firm handshake. "Thanks for coming to New York."

"Of course!" Jack nodded at the board members seated around the black-and-white marbled table. "It's good to see everyone in person."

Guillermo motioned for Jack to sit at the head of the table, where a bottle of water and a basket of snacks waited for him. *Nice,* he thought as he walked toward his chair. *This feels a bit more welcoming than our last board meeting. Good sign.*

"Jack," Renata said, smiling, "it's wonderful to have you here in person. It's been an exciting few months, right?"

"It has." Jack smiled back warmly. "Lots to report."

"Buddy!" Tom said, looking genuinely happy to see his old business school friend in person, "Welcome to the Big Apple! Looking forward to grabbing dinner tonight. Margo and the kids are excited to see you. Too bad Bridget couldn't make it."

"Yeah," Jack said, nodding. "Her job is as crazy as mine these days. She was bummed to miss this trip."

"Well, she's going to be pretty disappointed." Tom shook his head. "Margo and I picked a French restaurant that would be right up her alley."

"Ha!" Jack laughed. "She does love French food."

"Can we get you anything else before we begin? Coffee, tea?" Guillermo asked as he took the seat to Jack's left.

"Thanks. I'm fine with water." Jack pulled out his laptop and carefully placed it on the tabletop. Then he connected it to the projector in the center of the table. The large screen against the wall flickered for a second and then displayed the first slide of his presentation.

"Well then, let's get started." Guillermo sat back in his chair. "I know you have a presentation prepared, but before we get into that, I wanted to start with your financials. We had a chance to discuss and review the numbers you sent earlier this week. Looks like your team made progress."

Jack flipped to the financial summary slide in his presentation. "Yes, we met the ninety-day financial targets. Do you have specific questions I can answer for you?"

"How many of these strategic accounts did you close and how many did your team close?" Guillermo asked while studying the screen.

"I closed the ones in the first six weeks of the ninety-day period," Jack admitted. "But after we let go of Brett and brought in Steve, whom you all know from your work with him at other Gold companies, the sales team did the rest of the work and closed the latest round of strategic accounts. In the end, I'd say I closed about seventy percent and they closed about thirty percent."

"Not exactly the goal we discussed," Renata commented, glancing toward Guillermo for validation.

"Correct." Jack flipped to another slide. "But here's the sales pipeline as of yesterday. You can see that the team has built a decent pipeline that's getting stronger by the day. The team is well-positioned to execute on closing strategic accounts, and they're refocused. I believe we'll continue to see strong numbers from them and meet our revenue targets for the year."

"That's encouraging." Renata leaned forward in her chair. "Have you heard back on the offer you extended to the Chief Revenue Officer candidate we met?"

"Just this morning, actually." Jack smiled. "Erin Shin accepted our offer and will start in a few weeks."

"That's good!" Renata exclaimed. "We really liked her."

"I think she's going to make a huge difference." Jack opened his water bottle and took a sip. "Steve was great at stopping the bleeding, if you will. He was the right short-term choice to jump-start the sales team and focus them on penetrating strategic accounts in new verticals. But Erin is the leader we need to grow for the long term."

"And so, your focus is now on the transition?" Tom asked. "You gotta bring her in while continuing to deliver and without losing any momentum. And you can't afford to keep both Steve and Erin."

"Exactly." Jack turned to face his longtime friend. "Shauna, Steve, and I are meeting on Friday when I'm back in the office to develop a comprehensive plan. We budgeted up to a thirty-day transition period. I'm hoping we don't need that long, but we wanted to cover our bases."

Jack sat straight in his chair, hands folded on the table, ready for the next round of questions. But the team sat in silence for a few moments, only the distant sound of phones ringing echoing in the room.

Guillermo finally broke the silence. "Jack, this is good progress on the ninety-day objectives we laid out, but you know there's more to be done now, right?"

"Of course," Jack replied confidently. "I wanted to spend the bulk of our time today going through the overall organizational structure, the team, and some modifications I believe we need to make to deliver on our investment thesis."

Guillermo looked around the room to gauge the interest of the board, then returned his gaze to Jack. "We're intrigued. Please proceed."

Jack flipped through a few slides in his presentation until he found the one he wanted. "Over the last few weeks, I've had the opportunity to spend time with some of our new strategic accounts, and it got me thinking that even though we're a technology company, we've been operating as a services company. Today, we treat each new customer as its own project, and our team scopes out the requirements and builds something that works for the customer. But I think for us to really grow and meet our objectives, we need to operate more as what we really are—a software-as-a-service company, where we're selling a product and we're helping our customers customize it to what they need."

"It would definitely make you more efficient," Renata commented. "But is your technology ready for that?"

"It's close but not quite there," Jack replied. "I think we need to shift our focus to get it there. But I also think our existing team can't do this. Rob is phenomenal at technology, and he's come a long way in his transition to being a true CTO over the past few months. But he's not a product guy. I think we need a product leader to drive strategy and make sure our technology stays relevant to our customers in the long and short term."

"Have you thought about how Rob would work with a product leader?" Tom asked.

Jack turned to face Tom. "Yes, I think it would be a good pairing. A lot of the friction between Rob and Hannah happens because there isn't someone driving the product strategy. Hannah requests enhancements and bug fixes from Rob, and he decides how to prioritize them. Hannah gets caught flat-footed with the customer because she doesn't have a good product road map to share with them."

"It's definitely an interesting suggestion," Renata mused. "I think it would be a good test for Rob to see how he works with a product leader. He's made progress these last few months, but it's still too soon to tell if he's capable of being the type of modern CTO you're describing." Then she asked, "What other changes are you proposing?"

Jack flipped to another slide. "So, Hannah's doing a good job leading what I'll call a professional services organization, but I want her to focus on empowering the customer to adopt the product. I propose changing Hannah's title from COO to CCO, or Chief Customer Officer, with a singular focus on customer success across all verticals."

Tom leaned in so he could read the slide better. "Is it a semantic issue? I mean, aren't the customers her focus now?"

"Yes," Jack said, leaning back in his chair, "but she must figure out how to empower the customers to customize and adopt the product, not do it for them. It's a totally different skill set."

"Do you think she's capable?" Tom inquired.

"Yes, I do." Jack took a sip of water. "But I also know I will have to provide very clear performance objectives and coach her to success."

"I think highly of Hannah—she's delivered a lot of great results over the years. I think the key here will be to make sure you stay objective about her performance," Renata noted. "What about finance and HR? Any thoughts there?"

"You guys know Shauna is terrific, and she's been a wonderful partner to me since she's joined. She's amazing at the people stuff, feedback, and helping me to coach the leadership team, and I think she's developed a good understanding of our business." Jack flipped to another slide. "But our culture needs work, I don't feel like we have the right mindset to meet our growth objectives long term. I want her to really help me figure out the culture piece. I feel like we have a lot of work to do in this space, and I think it's a good growth area for her."

"I can see that. You have a lot of people from the old regime. They didn't have the growth objectives you face now. It will be tricky for you to change their mindset. But this new focus for Shauna is the right move for her growth and business growth, which is always a win," Tom commented. "What about Don?"

"Don has announced his intention to retire in eighteen months. I think our working relationship has improved over the past few months, and I've been impressed with his ability to be much more of a thought partner to me and the rest of the leadership team," Jack replied. "We're working on a succession plan for him, evaluating both internal and external candidates. I will keep you all apprised of our progress. Ideally, I'd like someone with SaaS experience as our next leader, so that may limit the internal candidates, but let's see."

Guillermo tapped his fingers on the desk while Tom fiddled with his stylus pen. Renata sat back in her chair and seemed to be processing.

Jack took slow breaths while he waited for the board to respond and made sure to keep a neutral expression on his face. He had worked so hard on this presentation with Meg, Steve, and Shauna and had actually been excited to get the board's feedback. But now, after going through it, the silence was deafening.

"Jack," Guillermo said, breaking the silence, "I have to say, this is good work. It's the type of thinking and ideas I'd expect a CEO to have. So, well done."

Jack felt a huge sense of relief wash over him. "Thank you."

"You're definitely moving in the right direction. I'd say you've gone from failing ninety-days ago to striving to get to where you need to be. You're not there yet, but you're making admirable progress at this point. I'm pleased," Guillermo said, leaning forward with a smile. "But now, you have to go from striving to thriving—and there's still a lot to do. Technically, Renata is right, you didn't quite meet the ninety-day objectives because you still closed the majority of the strategic accounts. That said, I'm sufficiently satisfied with the pipeline and the progress the team has made in a short period of time. We're going to be looking for you to continue this progress and make sure you don't micromanage when things go astray."

"I understand." Jack nodded. "I assure you, we're focused on getting to thriving," he said, getting the low rumble of amusement out of the board that he'd hoped for.

"We look forward to hearing more about your progress at our next board meeting." Guillermo stood up. "That's all I have. Enjoy the rest of your stay in New York."

Jack stood up and shook Guillermo's hand. "Thank you, I will."

Guillermo strode out of the room with several of the other board members right behind him. Tom high-fived Jack on his way out the double doors. Jack turned to Renata, who was still sitting in her chair, scrolling through her phone. "Renata, do you have a few minutes to chat?"

"Of course." She gestured for Jack to sit down and set her phone aside. "That was a good discussion. I could tell Guillermo was pleased, which isn't always easy to pull off. How do you feel?"

Jack took a sip of his water. "Energized. I am excited about where we are. I know we still have work to do, but I feel good about this path."

Renata smiled. "I'm glad. The last time we met, you didn't seem as confident as you did today."

"Well, it's in a large part to you," he acknowledged. "I wanted to thank you for introducing me to Meg and say I'm sorry I was so slow to accept the help."

Renata chuckled. "It's okay. You got there, which is the most important thing. I take it she was helpful?"

"Immensely!" Jack leaned back in his chair. "In addition to helping me get my head straight, she really helped me clarify my thinking about our operating model."

"Not surprised to hear it," Renata said. "I hope you're going to keep working with her. Like Guillermo said, there's still more to do to ensure you deliver results and win back the board's confidence."

"Yes, of course." Jack nodded. "I know I've still got a lot of work to do."

Renata smiled, gathered their things, stood up, and walked toward the doors. Before she exited the conference room, she stopped and turned around. "Good luck, Jack. We're all rooting for you. Let me know how I can help."

CHAPTER 19

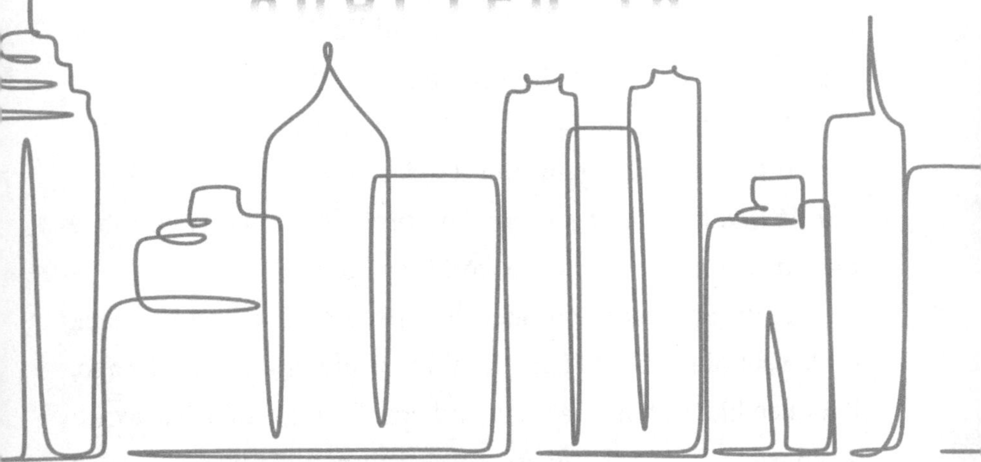

"THANKS AGAIN FOR a lovely dinner," Meg said as she leaned back in an oversize armchair and looked at the roaring fire in Jack's living room. "I didn't realize you were such a good cook!"

"That's kind of you, but I'm more of a functional cook. But I'm glad you liked my chicken divan." Jack handed her a Lager Libre. "I thought we could try some special craft beer you can only get in Atlanta. You said you like lagers, right?"

"Love lagers! I'm excited to try this." Meg studied the beer label before taking a sip. "Oh, that's yummy."

Jack sat down in the armchair next to her and said, "Glad we could make this work. Bridget and the kids loved meeting you."

"I loved meeting them. That Quinn is a spark plug!" Meg said, smiling.

"I know it. Three going on thirty." Jack shook his head. "I'm glad you came out to see Shauna and Ravi. They need all the support they can get. Were you able to see Sunil?"

Meg gave a slight nod. "He was okay, and he seems determined to fight this again. But it's clear the cancer has taken a toll. While his wit was there, he's probably down twenty-five pounds from when we were working together."

"Yeah, Shauna mentioned he's become quite weak." Jack took a sip of his beer. "I feel for that family. A few months ago, it looked like he had beaten it, and now for it to come back with a vengeance . . . well, I guess it feels so unfair." Then he looked at Meg. "I know what you're gonna say."

"What?" Meg looked surprised as she turned to face Jack. "What is it you think I'm going say?"

"That life is unfair."

"Well, as you know, in my view, it is." Meg shrugged her shoulders. "I just found that once I embraced that fact, I could stop dwelling on the unfair parts and focus on the things that really matter in a situation like this. I think of it as a coping mechanism."

Jack watched Meg scan the great room. The open layout was designed for entertaining. He and Bridget had made the most of the space, with an oversize sofa and throw pillows on the floor where people could sit, along with a few cozy spots for intimate conversations or reading. The traditional décor had a hint of casual comfort, which made it inviting and kid friendly. On the beige walls, they had framed several paintings of nature scenes—a mountainscape, a curved bridge in the middle of a forest, a river, and a farmhouse.

"Those paintings were done by a local artist," Jack commented. "We absolutely love her work."

"They're amazing!" Meg took a sip of her beer and then pointed at one of the family pictures carefully arranged on the mantel. "Is that you and your family in your office?"

Jack smiled. "Yes, that was the day my promotion became official. My predecessor, Chris, insisted on having my family there to mark the occasion. I love that picture—even have a copy of it in my downtown office. It always gives me a boost when I'm down or having a hard day."

"That's sweet." Meg smiled. "Tell me, when was the last time you had to look at it in your office? I hope it wasn't after your board meeting yesterday?"

"It's a been while for sure." Jack laughed. "I'm not gonna lie, there was a time I looked at it five times a day. Now it's more like once a month."

"Progress!" Meg raised her beer. "Seriously, though, how did yesterday's board meeting go?"

Jack took a long sip of his beer and stared at the fire for a few moments. He heard an echo of Bridget arguing with Jamie and Quinn about bedtime and wondered how long before she went into full drill sergeant mode with the kids.

"It was okay," Jack finally said. "These meetings go a bit better now, but we're not out of the woods. I'd describe the board as cautiously optimistic."

"That's good, right? Those Gold guys are tough. How do you feel?" Meg asked.

Jack placed his beer on the side table between the two armchairs, then stood up and threw a log in the fireplace. The fire raged and then settled into a steady crackling, a perfect salve for the early winter storm that had blown through and left a pocket of cold air hovering over the city for the last few days.

He could no longer hear any noises coming from upstairs. Bridget must have outmaneuvered the kids and finally got them into bed. He settled back into his armchair, picked up his almost empty beer, and stared at the fire for a bit.

"You know," Jack mused, "I definitely feel more energized, like we're on a good path transitioning to a SaaS company operating model. But it's interesting—while we've made good progress as a team, we're still not totally unified. The sales team is finally closing deals but not at the pace we need. We still haven't found a good product leader, which means I can't really change Hannah's role yet. It also means Rob and Hannah still get in each other's way and have to course correct."

"Are you having to step in with Rob and Hannah?" Meg asked, playing with her beer bottle. "You haven't mentioned it recently."

Jack shook his head. "No, I'm not the go-between anymore. They manage to work things out on their own. It just takes time."

"Well, that's progress!" Meg exclaimed.

"Yeah, it is." Jack swirled the beer in his bottle. "I just can't help feeling like we take two steps forward, one step back."

"Continue," Meg probed.

"Well, I just feel like our sales process is still not operating like a well-oiled machine."

"But Erin is doing well overall, right?" Meg inquired. "I mean, it sounded like she hit the ground running as the new sales leader, changing the company's sales incentives in her first few weeks. That took guts, right?"

"Yeah, that was a brazen move, but it was necessary." Jack took a sip of beer. "And she's done a good job communicating all the changes to the team. She's doing fine given her short tenure at the company, but as they say, old habits die hard. I think the sales team is still looking for the easy wins—but we're working on it."

Meg emptied her beer bottle. "Let me ask you a different question. Where did you expect you'd be at this point?"

Jack remained quiet for a bit, taking in the howling wind outside and the crackling fire inside.

"I guess I just thought we'd get to a place where we were only taking forward steps." Jack chuckled. "Probably too much to ask?"

"Ha! That's very optimistic." Meg laughed. "Besides, I'd definitely be out of a job if that were possible."

Jack pointed to Meg's bottle. "Another beer?"

"Thanks, but I have an early flight. How about some water?"

Jack nodded, picked up the two empty beer bottles, and made his way through the great room to the kitchen. He tossed the bottles in the recycling bin and pulled out two water bottles from the refrigerator. He strode back to great room, handed Meg a water, and settled back into the armchair.

"Not to get philosophical on you, but one of the hardest things to accept about life is that it's never a straight line," Meg said. "We might find balance for a few moments here and there, but mostly life is about navigating the ups and downs."

"That's true. Makes sense."

"So maybe consider your current circumstances from that point of view, knowing you will constantly be managing the ups and downs." She unscrewed the cap of the water bottle and took a sip. "Do you feel different than you did nine months ago?"

Jack contemplated Meg's question, remembering the relentless pressure he'd felt nine months ago—the constant frustration from his team and the feeling that he was letting everyone down. "Well, I don't feel like I'm being pulled in a million directions anymore. I'm not playing whack-a-mole," he said, chuckling. "I no longer dread board meetings or customer calls—and I no longer have that feeling that I'm letting everyone down. We have a plan, and we're getting there. I don't know, I feel stronger, more confident—like I'm more prepared to meet the constant challenges of my position. I guess you might say I'm more optimistic. I believe we're going to be okay." Then he paused, considering. "Do I feel different than I did nine months ago?" Jack grinned. "Yes, I do—completely!"

CHAPTER 20

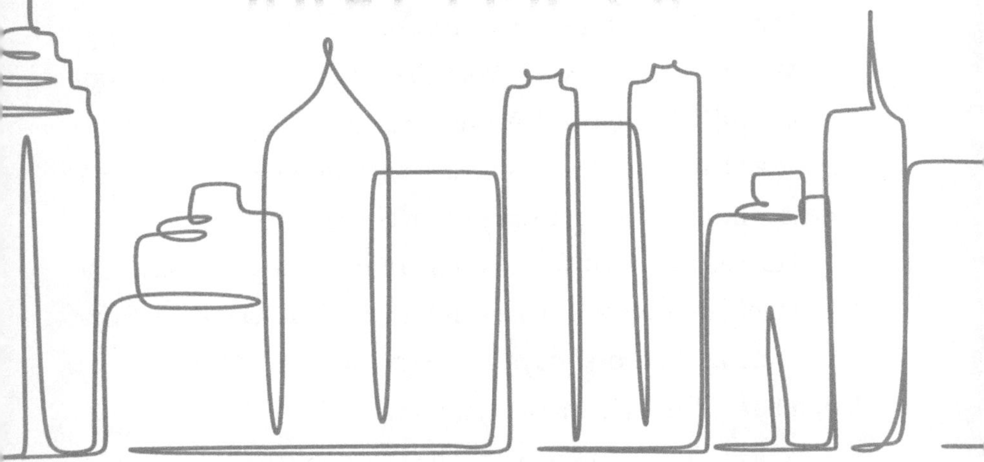

TWELVE MONTHS LATER
11:22 A.M.

"IT'S SO GOOD to see you again, Meg." Jack embraced his coach in a tight hug. "I just wish it were under better circumstances."

"Hi Jack," Meg said, returning his hug. "Can't believe it's been a year since we had dinner at your house."

"I know," Jack said as he stepped back. "Time is flying by, but it's my turn to come to California. I still dream about those burgers!"

"Anytime. I'd love to have dinner there with you again." Meg smiled. "Let me introduce you to a few folks. This is the

Dominal crew—Michelle Johnson, CEO; Mark Francis, former CEO and now chairman; and Jen Schmidt, COO. Everyone, this is Jack Shorn, CEO of Accelx and Shauna's current boss."

"Wow, it's great to meet all of you." Jack turned to shake each person's hand. "So glad you guys could make it to Atlanta to celebrate Sunil and support Shauna and Ravi."

"We wouldn't miss it," Michelle said as she firmly shook Jack's hand. "Those two have really been through the wringer these past two years. Sunil was such a terrific guy—we really got to know him and learn from him over the years."

"He was so insightful," Jen remarked, "and generous. And that laugh! It always warmed my heart. Shauna told me that even during the worst days of chemo, Ravi could still coax a laugh out of him. He was a joyful human."

"At least he got to know that he was going to be a grandfather." Mark tipped his punch glass toward a seven-month pregnant Shauna, who was chatting with family members across the room. "I'm just sorry he didn't get to meet his grandson."

"Meg, are you going to say something today?" Michelle asked.

Meg nodded. "Shauna asked me to write a poem to eulogize Sunil. I'll be reciting it at some point during the festivities."

"Looking forward to it." Jen raised a glass. "Your poetry always moves me."

"If it's anything like the few pieces you sent me, there won't be a dry eye in the room." Jack clinked glasses with Jen.

The five professionals stood in silence, sipping their drinks amid the buzz of the guests mingling in the ballroom. Shauna had prepped them all that while her father-in-law's celebration of life would start at eleven, the Indian crowd usually showed up a bit late, so they likely would serve lunch and start the program around noon.

"By the way, Jack," Mark started, "congratulations on winning portfolio company of the year last month. Shauna told us all about it. We're thrilled for you."

"Thanks!" Jack raised his glass. "And congratulations to all of you on your IPO—I'm so impressed with everything Dominal has accomplished. You guys are my idols."

"I don't know," Michelle said, "Dominal never won portfolio company of the year in all the time we were with Gold. You may be *our* idol."

"Let's find a table." Jen turned to Meg and Jack. "Will you guys join us?"

"We'd love to," Jack said, smiling. "Let's find a big one—the rest of our team is here floating around somewhere. I know they'd love to meet you guys. I just need two minutes with Meg, then I'll grab everyone and meet you there."

Michelle smiled. "We'll save your spots."

Mark, Michelle, and Jen made their way to an empty table, sat down, and placed their jackets and purses on the other open seats to hold them. Across the room, Jack and Meg found a quiet corner near a rectangular floor-to-ceiling window that looked out to a lush green landscape. While it was a somber occasion, there was still an upbeat feeling in the room, which Jack found consoling.

"I probably never shared this with you, but the Dominal team is the reason I am a full-time executive coach now. Those three over there really pushed me to pivot my business from fractional Chief People Officer services to executive coaching. I owe them a lot."

"Really? For some reason, I thought you went straight from corporate to coaching. Do you still work with them?"

"Nothing in my life has ever followed a straight line." Meg laughed. "Even my corporate career was meandering. But I digress. Yes, I still work with them."

"Were their initial issues similar to mine?" Jack asked.

Meg thought about Jack's question for a moment. "Not really. Dominal faced a threat from a third-party competitor and had to chart a comeback. I think you really needed to change up your leadership approach when you became CEO to position Accelx for success."

"I guess that's true," Jack admitted. "Well, I wanted to let you know our financials came in yesterday, and we had another record quarter. Erin has exceeded all my expectations on the sales front, plus she fits in so well with our leadership team. It feels like a totally different world now. Sure, we still have our ups and downs, but we're better prepared to handle them. I suppose I really did need to change things up. As they say, hindsight is always twenty-twenty, right?"

"That's wonderful!" Meg raised her glass. "I'm so proud of you."

"Thanks, it's a team effort." Jack clinked his glass to hers. "Speaking of teams, let's go find the rest of the team and sit down."

After a delicious Indian lunch of chicken tikka, basmati rice, spinach paneer, roasted eggplant, and garlic naan, the eulogies began. After a few speeches from Sunil's family, a visibly nervous Shauna strode on to the stage and picked up the microphone.

"Hi everyone. For those of you who don't know me, my name is Shauna Miller-Desai. For the last five years, I've had the privilege of introducing myself as Sunil's daughter-in-law, because I am married to his eldest son, Ravi."

Shauna gave a hint of a smile, her hand trembling slightly. She seemed to be willing herself to hold it together.

"Over lunch, you heard about Sunil as a family man—a father, husband, and brother. I'm here to share that he was also an amazing father-in-law and professional mentor. From the moment Ravi introduced me to his father, Sunil welcomed me with open arms and an open heart. He treated me like a daughter, and I loved him like a father. For that, I will always be grateful."

Shauna's voice cracked, and she tightened her grip on the microphone. "Sunil was the CEO of Elastitech for ten years. He was an amazing leader. He started as a programmer and, over the course of his career, worked his way through many management and leadership roles, ultimately going from CTO to CEO. He imparted so many valuable lessons, which I think helped me become a stronger leader myself and, more importantly, a better human. I wanted to share some of his wisdom with you today." She paused to take a deep breath before continuing.

"When Ravi and I were dating, I noticed that people would ask Sunil how it felt to be a successful CEO. His response was always the same." Shauna mimicked her father-in-law's deep Indian accent as she said, "'I don't know. I'll tell you when I get there.'" The audience gave a soft, collective laugh. Everyone was smiling and nodding knowingly, remembering Sunil's profound humility.

"Sunil's statement perplexed me at first," Shauna continued in her own voice. "Elastitech had grown so much under his leadership, how could he not believe he was successful?" Shauna focused her gaze on Jack as she asked the question. "So, I asked him about it one day, and he told me that in his experience, success was fleeting. You could enjoy moments of success, but you couldn't let it define you. Success, he said, wasn't a destination—and anyone who told you so was either lying or about to fall into a chasm. Real success, he said, was measured in persistence, grit, and the ability to work through the next challenge, which is always just around the corner. Leadership, in work and in life, is about walking the very fine line between being kind, grateful, compassionate, and being honest with people when things aren't working. It's about hard work and difficult decisions and conversations. And when you have to sit with those difficult decisions and conversations—and you're at your lowest—real success is about resilience and finding the courage to get back up and keep leading." She wiped away a few tears before continuing. "He reminded me often that significant growth comes from failures and mistakes." She slipped back into her Sunil impression and said, "'For every success, Shauna, there will be at least ten failures and missteps. *This* is what real leadership looks like on the job and in life.'"

Shauna scanned the room until she found Michelle. "Sunil believed that integrity was doing what you said and saying what you will do. He practiced this principle every day, which inspired everyone around him and built a strong bond of trust among his people and his family. His impeccable character created a culture of innovation and collaboration—both necessary for the type of high-performance growth that became the norm at Elastitech during his tenure. For Sunil, life might not always have been easy, but the principles that guided him at home and work were simple and irrefutable. Do your best and do the right thing all the time, even when no one is watching."

She exhaled and then focused her gaze on Meg. "You see, through his work and the way he lived his life, Sunil embodied each and every principle our longtime coach and friend Meg Beecham describes as modern leadership."

Shauna took out a tissue, dabbed her eyes, and tried a smile. "The world has lost a very special human. I will miss Sunil with all my heart for the rest of my life. I am especially sad that he won't be with us to share his wonderful life and leadership lessons with our son." Her voice cracked. "But I am heartened to see so many leaders in my life who abide by these same principles, many of whom are here today, including Mark Francis, Michelle Johnson, Jen Schmidt, and of course, my current boss, Jack Shorn, who has always shown me and my family such grace and respect, particularly over these past twelve months. Sunil's legacy lives on through all of you."

Tears ran down Shauna's face, and Ravi walked up and enveloped her in a hug. Keeping his arm around his wife, he gently took the mic from her hand.

"Honey, that was amazing. Thank you. If Dad were here, he'd be very proud of you." He kissed her cheek. "Everyone, we'll take a short break while we serve dessert and then continue with the program."

Meg wiped her eyes and turned to the table. "That was such a lovely tribute to Sunil and each of you."

Mark smiled and raised his glass. "Here's to Sunil!"

"To Sunil!" They all toasted to the sound of clinking stemware.

Meg turned to Jack. "You sure got a big mention from Shauna. How do you feel?"

"Embarrassed!" Jack exclaimed. "But it was very sweet. Did you see her focusing her gaze on each of your clients with each lesson?"

Meg shook her head. "No! I think that was in your imagination. She was just looking across the audience."

The waiter came by and placed plates of Sunil's favorite dessert, chocolate cheesecake, in front of each of them. Another waiter followed and filled their cups with piping hot coffee.

"Imagination or not, Meg, you've definitely made an impact on a lot of leaders. I can't thank you enough for everything you've done and continue to do for us at Accelx." Jack took a big bite of cheesecake.

"Aw, thanks," Meg said, beaming. "You know I'm always here for you. But you're the one who does the work. I just provide guidance and feedback. It's been such a pleasure to watch your growth. You're the star. I'm just cheering you on from the audience."

"Well, be that as it may, thanks for everything." Jack smiled and raised his coffee cup to his mentor. "And may you always have a front row seat."

ACKNOWLEDGEMENTS

THANK YOU FOR taking the time to read this book. For me, writing fiction is a fun and creative challenge, and I love hearing how my stories influence and impact people's lives. Writing a book is a team effort, and I wanted to acknowledge the people who have stood by me in the two-year journey to get this book across the finish line.

First and foremost, I want to thank my editor and good friend, Kathy Meis. We've now worked together on two books. She encourages me to challenge myself as an author and was extremely patient as we reworked the premise of this book a few times to get it to where it is today. Her guidance was invaluable during the writing process.

Next, I'd like to thank my family, who always shows up and supports me in any endeavor I take on. Life has different seasons and over the last two years, my family and I have experienced some very tough and unexpected losses. I want to thank my friends for helping me through these challenging times and taking on some of the load when it was too heavy for me to carry by myself.

I'd also like to thank all the beta readers who took time to read this book and provide in-depth feedback as well as all my clients—past and present—who enrich my life in so many ways. There is no greater gift a coach can experience than watching people grow and achieve their full potential. I'm so honored to be a small part of their journey.

Finally, I'd like to share the poem I wrote for my aunt Shama Jani, who passed away from glioblastoma in March 2023. She was one of the most creative people I'd ever met and was so proud when I published my first book. I know she would have been thrilled about this one too. Meg's poetic tribute to Sunil mirrored this poem.

THE PRESENTS

On a gloriously warm spring day
In 1953 on the nineteenth of May
A gift of the purest form of love
Showered the earth from up above
When a tender and delightful soul
Joined the world to make it whole.

In early years this gift would cultivate
Until the time came for us to relate.
Once we basked in its distinctive glow
Our life developed a melodious flow
As this gift framed a subliminal view
Of the journey we traveled through.

As life took this gift down a bleak road
It never stopped to dwell on the load
Rather it renewed its spirit in living
And this exquisite gift kept on giving
Through an arduous and sinuous trail
Enlightening us on how to boldly prevail.

When it was time for the gift to depart
A gaping hole formed in my wistful heart
Craving the warmth of our unique gift.
Through our memories I continue to sift
Until I spot two presents it left behind
In them, it's her precious love we find.

SEE HOW IT ALL BEGAN...

CHAPTER 1

MARK FRANCIS, CEO of Dominal Industries, stood alone in his corner office late on a Monday afternoon and stared out intently at the brown trees and gray sky. He lightly banged his forehead against the large window.

It had been an unseasonably cold fall in Chicago. Even now, in early September, some trees had already shed leaves, revealing the first barren branches of autumn.

Mark shuddered, turning from the window to see financial reports strewn across the mahogany executive desk of the retired Dominal chairman and founder, George Jordan.

He stretched to get the kink out of his neck, recalling how proud George had been when he'd gifted the desk to Mark in celebration of his promotion to CEO eighteen months ago.

Since its founding in 1995, Dominal Industries had been a powerhouse, pioneering and manufacturing components required for health management machines, such as insulin pumps and blood pressure monitors. For more than twenty years, the Jordan family had held tight reins on the business, innovating both its product and business model to continue its domination of the market. Mark was the first leadership hire outside the Jordan family and was brought in to help George retire and sell the company.

Mark turned back toward the window. He had spent the better part of the afternoon going through the latest financial projections with Allan Chang, the chief financial officer for Dominal Industries, and reviewing the reports again by himself.

The news was not good.

Mark's office phone began to ring—once, twice, three times—but he stood perfectly still, focused on his breathing, and continued to stare out the window. A few moments later, there was a soft knock at the office door. His assistant peeked in. "Mark, it's Renata Campbell for you."

Renata Campbell, the managing partner for Gold Private Equity, had orchestrated the deal for Gold to buy Dominal Industries.

"Thanks. Please put her through." Mark moved slowly back toward his desk and sat down in his Herman Miller chair. He inhaled deeply and picked up the phone. "Hello, Renata. How are you?"

"Hi, Mark. I'm fine, thanks for asking." There was a slight echo as Renata was on speakerphone. "Hey, I know you're busy, but I need a few minutes of your time."

"Of course." Mark rubbed his forehead, preparing for the worst.

"I'm calling about the upcoming board meeting. I just want to give you a little insight on the internal discussions the investors are having."

Mark knew what was coming. He pictured Renata standing at her lightly stained maple desk, smoothing her straight black hair in the Wacker Drive high-rise office building that Gold occupied. He braced himself.

"Look, I know you've seen the numbers. The investors are going nuts. To put it bluntly, they're shitting their pants."

Mark's shoulders tensed. "Yeah, we're going through the details here. I know it looks bad, but I'm on it—"

"Mark," Renata said, cutting him off, "you've got to drive real results to turn this around. This has to be the best damn plan the board has ever seen, and you need to make sure you execute it flawlessly."

"I get it. There are definitely some additional cuts we can make to help profitability in the short term to show immediate impact."

"That's not enough. You need to be more deliberate and thoughtful in your actions to regain the board's confidence.

They're concerned that your team isn't focused on the right things."

Mark rose from his chair. "What do you mean?"

"Your sales strategy is unclear, operations seem inefficient, turnover is abysmal, and you still haven't hired a head of R&D yet. For God's sake, it's been twelve months!"

"I know. We've been out recruiting, but it's a tough market." Mark began pacing as far as his phone cord would allow.

"C'mon, Mark, you know that won't stand up. Xtele is making huge inroads into the market with cheaper versions of our products while probably building the next big thing, and you're blaming a tough recruiting market? Really?"

Mark ran his fingers through his wavy brown hair, which had just started graying at the temples—the only physical indication that he'd turned fifty earlier this year. Again, he stared out the big window.

"Look, you know I believe in you. I was the one who pushed the investors hard to promote you to CEO, remember? I convinced the other board members that you were ready to deliver the high performance that we needed, even though you had been the COO for such a short time. I also fought hard for you when you barely missed last year's targets."

Mark picked up his Boston Red Sox stress ball and rolled his eyes, having heard this reminder many times before. "Okay, what do I have to do to gain the rest of the board's confidence?"

"Get your leadership team focused, and do it now. This first quarter was a total disaster, and it's only going to get worse. You gotta fix this. This is your last chance. Do you understand?"

"Yes, I do. I assure you." Mark mustered all the confidence he could. "I promise, we'll demonstrate how we're going to turn this around at the next board meeting."

Mark hung up the phone, dropped back into his chair, and planted his head face down on the desk. A faint, dull roar could be heard from the adjacent building where machines churned out Dominal's product twenty-four hours a day. He suddenly felt nauseated.

The leadership team Mark had carefully built over the past eighteen months were all hard-working, committed professionals. Though they hadn't quite found their rhythm as a team yet, all the essential components were there. Some of the new leadership team members had left steady, good-paying jobs to take a chance with Dominal.

Then there were the 2,500 employees, some with more than twenty years of service. Their lives would be totally disrupted if Dominal had to be sold at a loss or started to lay people off.

Mark thought about his wife, Leanne, and their three kids. A lump rose in his throat. They'd never complained about having to sell their perfect Greystone home after he left Davis & Edwards and decided to take some time off. Leanne had stepped up in so many ways.

Mark cleared his throat and straightened up in his chair. He once again inhaled, held, and then exhaled. Suddenly, a flood of fresh ideas began to fill his head. He started typing like a madman.

A brief, loud knock interrupted Mark's flow.

Jen Schmidt, Dominal's chief human resources officer, opened the door and stepped in. "Hey, Mark. Do you have a minute?"

Mark nodded but continued staring at his monitor. Jen closed the door behind her and made her way over to the far end of his desk. She crossed her arms and stood for a moment, apparently hoping he would make eye contact.

"I wanted to let you know we just settled the Palmer case. He signed the severance agreement without incident. He accepted our first offer, which never happens. We're quite pleased with the outcome, and I thought you'd want to know." Jen gave Mark a satisfied smile.

"Uh, thanks, Jen," Mark murmured without removing his eyes from the screen.

Jen subtly cleared her throat. He didn't respond, trying to make it clear she was not going to get any further reaction from him on this issue. Just as she started to make her way to the door, Renata's words about the open positions echoed in Mark's head.

He snapped his head away from the monitor. "Hey, Jen, hold up a sec. How's the R&D search?"

Jen turned around from the middle of Mark's office, surprised. "We just discussed this in our last check-in. The team has been pounding the pavement."

"Okay, but do we have any new candidates?"

"No, we don't." Jen sighed and tilted her head. "It's a very tough market. We're doing everything we can."

"Are we, Jen? Are we really doing *everything* we can? It's been twelve months!" Mark blinked hard, feeling the pressure build up behind his eyes.

Jen took a few steps toward Mark's desk. "I've kept you in the loop the whole time. What more do you think we could be doing?"

"I don't know. Our competitors are out in the market building the next big thing—meanwhile, we can't even get one decent candidate in the door!"

"Mark, to be fair, you cut ten percent of our budget last year. I think I'm doing a pretty good job of doing more with less. I'm not sure what else we can do."

"You need to come up with something!" Mark shot up from his chair. "It's your job to get this role filled."

"Okay, then." Jen's hazel eyes looked past Mark at the steady drizzle outside of his office window. She straightened her tan suit. "Well, let me think through some options and get back to you."

"Wait, hang on." Mark held his hand up and slumped back into his chair. He motioned for her to sit down. He closed his eyes and rubbed his forehead. "You know, Jen, I just never thought we'd be here. We were at the top of our game when George sold eighteen months ago . . . and then, *boom.* Xtele just comes at us from out of nowhere. Now we're fighting to stay alive."

Jen shifted uncomfortably in her chair.

"Look, I've been meaning to talk to you." Mark folded his hands on his desk. "You know I believe in you, and you've done some really good work over the past year—including coaching me and other leaders through some difficult conversations and employee issues. Everyone at Dominal feels that you're approachable. We all feel you have a lot of potential . . ."

Jen sat perfectly still, staring at the beige carpet.

"I know we've asked you to do more with less, and you never push back. But lately, it feels like you're not focused on the right things. I think you need help rethinking your approach."

Jen's head jolted up. "I'm not sure I understand."

"Well, you know how you always talk about coaches for our high-potential leaders who just need some guidance, right?"

Jen nodded.

"Well, now it's your turn. I just learned about this consultant named Meg Beecham. She comes highly recommended from many people I trust in my network. She has a totally different approach to HR. Give her a business problem, and she develops a people solution. That's what you need." Mark handed Jen a business card.

"Okay." Jen accepted the card with a bemused look.

"I haven't had a chance to talk to her. Just make an appointment with her this week."

"With all due respect," Jen began, seeming to snap out of her trance, "I've got years of experience, and it's not like I'm new to Dominal."

"Yes, you're right. And your experience has been invaluable to us in many ways. I also believe you are the right person to lead HR long term, but we're stuck right now. The board is all over us about turnover and key positions going unfilled for too long. It's killing us. We need a fresh perspective if we're going to stay alive. These are HR challenges—*your* challenges—and I think you could use some help taking a different approach."

Jen sighed. "It doesn't sound like I have a choice."

"Well, the reality is we have to start thinking differently if we're going to get ahead of Xtele. We need to get these problems under control, and fast. Meg can help."

CHAPTER 2

MEG BEECHAM STOOD in the hallway across from the hotel ball-room, adjusting the satchel bag on her shoulder. She smoothed her black jeans and pulled at the cuffs of her white blouse, which were accented with little embroidered sunflowers. She sighed and started to plod her way toward the hotel bar, exhausted from her talk.

She turned right, passing through a charming hallway lined with small, inviting conference rooms. This old hotel, which stood in the heart of Chicago, was one of her all-time favorites. She'd been thrilled when the conference sponsors chose such a unique location. The hotel retained so much of its original look and feel—a timeless feel that she absolutely loved.

At precisely three in the afternoon, Meg arrived at the entrance of the nearly empty hotel bar. She loved this watering hole right in the middle of the hotel's historic lobby. The dimly lit room with a long, oversized oak bar from 1910 was the perfect place to take in a few craft beers and contemplate the bigger questions of life. It reminded her of the old pubs she'd frequented on her last trip to the English countryside.

The grand fireplace on the back wall spewed roaring flames, a perfect invitation to warm up at the end of a long autumn day. Out of the corner of her eye, Meg saw a woman sitting at a table near the back. Mid-thirties, shoulder-length brown hair, wearing a tailored black pantsuit, cream silk blouse, and black stilettos. The woman's eyes were scanning the room anxiously. Meg figured this must be her prospective client.

"Hi . . . Jennifer?"

The woman stood up, looking slightly confused at the casually dressed woman in front of her. She reached out her hand. "Uh . . . yes . . . Meg? Please, call me Jen. Thanks for making time for me."

Even though Meg's black boots gave her two extra inches, Jen was still quite a bit taller than her.

"No worries, Jen it is. I'm glad we were able to make this work." She put her bag down on the empty chair between them. "I actually just finished my talk a few minutes ago," Meg went on, taking a seat in the three-legged antique chair across from Jen.

"How did it go?"

Meg shrugged and gave a tired smile. "I think it went okay. Hard to tell." She picked up the small, laminated bar menu and studied it for a few seconds, then abruptly put it down, inclined her head slightly, and looked Jen straight in the eyes. "I know we just met, but can I ask you a favor?"

Jen blinked and jerked her head back. "Uh, sure, I guess."

"So, I'm not the best at giving these keynotes. I mean, I practice hard, but it still just takes it out of me. So, right now, I am *totally* spent. Could you please be patient with me today, you know, if I'm a little slow?"

"Not a problem." Jen chuckled. "I'm a working mother of two kids under six. I'm always running near empty. I completely understand."

Meg smiled. "I appreciate it." She tried to decide whether Jen matched the image in her head but was interrupted by the waiter.

"What can I get you two to drink today?"

"I'll take a Daisy Cutter Pale Ale, please. Jen, how about you?"

"Well, uh, I don't usually start drinking at three . . . but if you're having a beer, I guess I'll have a glass of the house white wine. Thank you."

"Love that you're willing to bend the rules," Meg exclaimed.

Jen smiled weakly. "When did you arrive in Chicago, Meg?"

"I actually came in over the weekend and took in a game at Wrigley Field."

Jen perked up. "Are you a baseball fan?"

The waiter arrived back at the table and quietly served their drinks.

"Not really. Back in LA, I have this friend who's a big Cubs fan . . . always going on about how great they are. I figured the least I could do was go to a game while I was here."

"I'm a huge Cubs fan, myself. Still get goosebumps when I think about the 2016 World Series. Sometimes my husband Dave and I rewatch Game 7 just to relive the magic."

"To the Cubs." Meg raised her mug to Jen. "My friend does the same thing and still tears up at the end. Who knew there could be so much history from a goat? What a game! I mean, how they came back from that rain delay . . . yeah, that was pretty cool."

Meg lifted her beer to eye level as she spoke, studying its color more closely. "It's a shame we don't get this beer at home." She took a satisfying slurp. "Well, here's to the next 108 or so years! Hopefully you don't have to wait that long again!"

"I'll drink to that!" Jen laughed and took her first sip of wine. "And I hope we have another successful postseason. You know, it's starting soon!"

Meg pulled up the sleeves of her blouse. "So, why do you think your boss asked you to reach out to me?"

"I'm not really sure. He just says he wants a different . . ." Jen's eyes grew large, and she stared at Meg's left wrist. "Sorry, I don't mean to be rude, but is that a tattoo?"

"Oh, yeah." Meg's blue eyes glanced down at her wrist. "It's Japanese kanji. Reminds me to be creative every day in order to be my best self."

"That's so cool!" Jen leaned over Meg's arm like a curious child. "What's your main creative outlet?"

"I write poetry," Meg replied. "I'm not published or anything . . . it's just a hobby. What about you? Do you have free time?"

"Very little," Jen admitted. "But I do love to paint. I've been drawing and painting my whole life. Not as much lately, though. I miss it."

"Any special type of painting?"

"Yes, I'm all about oil painting." Jen's hazel eyes brightened. "I love to take everyday sights and change the perspective of them through unique angles, colors, and shadows. It takes some thought and practice, but I find it really stimulating."

"Good for you. I find artistic people look at situations from different perspectives and typically offer more creative solutions."

"Interesting. I hadn't really thought about it that way." Jen took a sip of her wine.

"How's your wine?"

"Actually, not bad for a house. I think it's a sauvignon blanc." Jen glanced around the room. "This place is pretty cool. I've never been here before. My husband, Dave, would love it."

"Yeah, it's one of my favorite places in Chicago. A hidden gem." Meg felt a foam mustache forming on her upper lip and wiped her mouth with her napkin. "Great craft beer selection."

"Dave loves beer of all types, but when we go out, he likes to try different craft beers. I'm sure he'll want to come here for our next date night." Jen rolled her eyes. "So much for romance."

Meg laughed. "What does Dave do?"

"He's a finance director for an engineering firm. I give him a hard time about it, of course, but he's a great guy. He's been taking care of the kids a lot lately while I've been focused on work." Jen sipped her wine. "What about you? Married?"

"Not anymore," Meg said. "It was great while it lasted, but I think I'm just one of those people who does better alone."

"Marriage certainly isn't for everyone," Jen said softly, "but good for you for realizing what works best for your life."

"Thanks. Not many people understand."

Jen nodded, and they were both silent for a few moments.

"So, how did you end up at Dominal Industries?" Meg asked.

"Well, I worked with Allan, our CFO, early in my career at this company called Leal & Franklin. It was a professional services firm." Jen sipped her drink. "He was the finance manager back then. We stayed friends after we left, and he introduced me to Dominal shortly after it got sold to Gold."

"A strong relationship with the CFO is key." Meg acknowledged. "Tell me more about your background."

She listened intently as Jen traced her background, from graduating at the top of her class at the University of Illinois at Urbana–Champaign to taking on progressive roles in recruiting and HR in a variety of different industries—financial services, professional services, and tech.

"Your background is impressive. You've had some pretty significant roles, and it sounds like you've made a difference at every company."

"Thanks. I've worked hard, but also believe some of it was being in the right place at the right time."

"So, tell me a little more about what Dominal is facing now?"

"Well, we've recently been hit by a Chinese competitor that is quickly gaining market share." Jen pushed back a few strands of her brown hair that were in her face. "Our first-quarter financial performance was terrible, and our full-year projections don't look so great either. My boss, Mark, who's also the CEO, is pretty stressed out. It sounds like our board is all over him."

"I bet, that's a tough spot. What's your HR team like?"

"We have a good team—about ten people, including recruiters. We had to make cuts last year, but we've managed to make it work." Jen played with the damp cocktail napkin upon which her wine glass was resting. "So, maybe you could tell me a little about your background, Meg?"

"Sure. Well, I have over twenty-five years of experience. I started my career in IT and then took on roles in finance, strategy, and HR. I've had a few executive roles at a national bank and was a global talent executive at a Fortune 500 before starting my own company."

"Wow!" Jen exclaimed. "That's great—and pretty unique. I'm not sure I've ever met a finance person who can write poetry."

"You probably have, they just won't admit to it." Meg smirked. "People's talents are surprising when they let you see them."

"And what does your company do, exactly?" Jen sipped her wine slowly.

"Well, it's just me, and I left the corporate world to pursue this passion I have for helping companies think differently about HR—you know, move it away from its focus on compliance. I believe it's time to modernize the way HR functions, driving more growth and creating a place where people love to work." Meg straightened up in her chair. "So, I mostly advise CEOs on people strategies and programs to help them get there. Think of me as a fractional chief people officer."

"Interesting. But what if a company already has a chief people officer?" Jen sat up a bit and folded her hands in her lap.

"Don't worry, I'm not here to compete or take anyone's job. I promise. I'm here to add value. From time to time, I work with HR professionals, too, if that makes sense."

"So, you work alongside them?" Jen surmised.

"Yes, or end up translating between HR and the CEO, who aren't always aligned. I help get everyone on the same page."

"Do you focus on any specific industries or company size?"

"I'm industry agnostic—anything and everything from manufacturing to Bay Area tech startups. I do tend to focus on middle-market and emerging-growth organizations—a lot of investor-backed companies."

"Interesting." Jen rolled back her shoulders. "Like us. So, tell me more about how you work with clients?"

"What do you mean?"

"Well, do you have a process or methodology or program you follow?"

"Not really." Meg folded the edge of her cocktail napkin. "I mean, you know from your experience that every business is unique."

"True," Jen acknowledged. "But surely you have a standard approach?"

"I guess my approach is to understand the business challenges and then figure out the gaps. From there, I come up with a people solution. That's the only way you can drive better outcomes."

"Hmm . . ." Jen wore a puzzled expression. "Do you have an example?"

"I recently had a client who'd missed their operating targets for a few years. When we dug into it, their performance management system seemed disconnected from their business goals. Each year, over eighty-five percent of their employees were getting a 'meets expectations' or higher, even though the entire company was missing its operating targets. I helped them redesign their approach. This past year, their performance management results matched their business results, and, more importantly, they hit their goals."

"Yeah." Jen exhaled deeply. "We face a similar challenge. It's on my list to tackle eventually, but I'm not sure I've ever looked at things that way."

"Yes, it does take a different kind of thinking." Meg took a swig of beer. "But that's usually why I'm brought in."

"Well, that's intriguing. But I just don't know that I agree with Mark that this is the best way for me to be spending my time given current pressures."

"Hmm." Meg tilted her head. "What do you think would be a better use of your time?"

"I'm not sure." Jen sighed. "It's not you, Meg, it's just that I feel like I should be able to do what Mark is asking. I have years of HR experience. It's not like I'm new to the job."

"It's not a sign of weakness to bring in help." Meg swirled the remaining beer in her glass. "As a matter of fact, it's really a sign of strength. We all hit roadblocks no matter how much experience we have, right? And often a little help or a different perspective is what enables us to move forward."

"Yeah, I guess you're right."

Meg finished the last of her beer and put the glass down with a slight thud. "Look, I think I can help you and your team get focused on the key things you need to do to enable business growth."

Jen cast her eyes around the crowd gathering at the bar. The room had started to get noisy, and it was becoming hard for them to hear each other. A small group of conference attendees waved at Meg when they walked past their table. Jen studied Meg's expression when she waved back.

"Can I just say, you look exhausted."

"Ha, thanks, kind of you to notice." Meg nodded. "I *do* need some sleep—maybe on the flight home tomorrow—but I would like to continue this conversation. I'd love the opportunity to help."

"Okay." Jen swallowed her last sip of wine. "But I gotta warn you, between work and family, there's not a lot of extra time. I'll try my best."

"I understand. We'll do the best we can with the hours you have. I'd never want you to miss family time. That's not something you can ever get back."

"I appreciate that."

"One last thought before you go: I do things a bit differently. I hope that's okay."

"You don't say?" Jen cocked her head and smiled. "The finance–poetry combo was a dead giveaway."

"Yeah." Meg chuckled. "After I left corporate, I shed a lot of layers, but it's made me better at what I do. Have you ever heard of the movie *The Karate Kid*?"

"From the '80s? Yeah, I think I saw it when I was a kid."

"Likely. It's a classic, right? I loved it but forgot about it for years. Then, when I went out on my own, something brought me back to it. I ask every client to watch it. Are you open to this? I warned you I do things a bit differently."

"Ha. Sure, I guess."

"Great," Meg replied, smiling. "You can find it on one of the streaming services. Let me know when you've watched it, and we'll find a time to get started."

"Okay, sounds good." Jen gathered her purse.

Meg slung her satchel over her shoulder, shook Jen's hand, and the two women started walking toward the elevators. "Thanks again for coming out. I look forward to talking again soon. And thanks for understanding how tired I am. I was re-energized by our conversation."

"My pleasure," Jen said, stepping into the antique elevator that Meg knew headed toward the garage.

Directly across from her, Meg stepped into another elevator and headed up to her floor. She couldn't wait to order room service and hit the sack.

CHAPTER 3

JEN'S CELL BUZZED wildly on the particle board desk in her windowless office while she held her landline to her ear, waiting for Shauna to answer. She quickly picked it up and saw a string of text messages from Mark. It was only nine a.m., and she had already taken a few calming breaths given the craziness of the morning. Jen needed her head of HR operations, and *fast*. She tapped her pen on the desk rapidly while she waited.

Her cell phone buzzed again. She sighed, seeing it was a text from Allan: *Are you on your way? Mark's anxious.*

Jen texted back a thumbs-up emoji, hopeful that her long-time friend could placate Mark until she could get to the meeting. She closed her eyes and said a silent prayer that Shauna would pick up her phone soon.

Then, at last, Shauna picked up. "This is Shauna."

"Shauna, finally! Hey, remember what happened the last time there was an accident at the facility?"

Jen's cell buzzed again.

"Crap, Mark and Allan keep texting. I'm totally late for our leadership meeting. Anyway, remember how benefits misfiled the paperwork, and it cost the company a ton of money?" Jen played with the Wrigley Field paperweight on her desk while she listened to Shauna's response. "That's right, Shauna. Perfect. Yes, I need you on this immediately. Promise me you won't let history repeat itself, okay? Thanks. Gotta run."

Jen hung up the landline, grabbed her cell phone and a folder full of papers, and sprinted in her stilettos down the long, narrow hallway that showcased every award Dominal had ever won. She made her way past Mark's and Allan's offices, took a sharp right at the end of the hallway, and rushed into the board room just as Allan was presenting his department's latest projections. She stumbled slightly as she neared her place at the twenty-foot white marble conference table that dominated the rarely used formal meeting room that George Jordan had insisted on during the last office remodel. Allan picked up the papers that had slid out of Jen's folder and onto the beige carpet. He gave Jen a reassuring look when he handed them back to her.

"Ah, Jen, late as usual!" Rich Peters, Dominal's head of sales, interrupted as Jen regained her balance.

Mark shot Rich a stern look. "Everything okay, Jen?"

She adjusted her gray suit blazer. The large windows in the boardroom let in the bright, fall morning sunlight. Jen squinted a bit as she sat down.

"Yes. Sorry I'm late." Jen smiled insincerely at Rich. "There was an accident in the facility, and one of the supervisors was taken to the hospital. I was on the phone making sure benefits prepares the paperwork correctly this time." She turned to Mark. "That's why I couldn't pick up your call. I just didn't want to repeat that costly mistake we made last year."

"What's the name of the supervisor who was hurt?" Mark wore a concerned expression. "Is he okay? What happened?"

"Peter Morrill. Um, he's a . . ." Jen flipped through her papers. "Well, uh, I don't have a lot of details about his condition yet. I believe he was stable and alert when the ambulance left." Jen noticed everyone exchanging perplexed looks.

Allan leaned forward in his chair as though he was about to say something, when Michelle Johnson, Dominal's chief operations officer, jumped in.

"Peter is one of our shift supervisors. He's going to be fine. Apparently, there was an issue with the new honing machine, and he fell while evaluating the problem. Thankfully, Jerry was right there when it happened and reacted quickly to keep everyone calm and follow our safety procedures. I called his wife and plan to stop by the hospital on my way home."

Jen gave Michelle a quick smile, grateful for her support. They were hired around the same time and got along well both professionally and personally. They enjoyed an occasional drink after work to discuss the ins and outs of juggling motherhood, work, husbands, and the Cubs.

"Thanks, Michelle." Mark tapped his pen on the table. "Could you also give me his wife's number? I want to call after the meeting and offer my personal support to the family. I will also stop by the facility after this meeting and thank Jerry personally."

"That would be great. I know his wife would appreciate it. She was a bit nervous when I talked to her. I can't imagine getting a phone call like that." Michelle sighed. "But even she was relieved when I told her that Jerry was right there. I gotta tell you, I've worked with a lot of ops guys in my twenty years, and Jerry is by far the best director of logistics I've had the pleasure of meeting. We're really lucky to have him."

"For sure," Jen added. "I'll send flowers on behalf of Dominal."

Everyone seemed to contemplate Peter's predicament quietly for a few moments.

Mark broke the silence. "Okay, please keep us posted on Peter. Let's get back to it for now. Allan, can you please pick up where you left off?"

Allan returned to presenting projections and explaining how his team was partnering with sales and operations to improve performance.

"Allan, I assume your projections include the reductions we made last year in HR?" Jen pointed to the numbers on the page. "Those were pretty substantial, but we're committed to doing our part, even if it means we have to run lean."

Allan gave Jen a friendly nod. "It's all there."

Rich shared the progress of the new sales channels his team had identified and how he was driving performance across the sales territories. He once again highlighted the pricing pressure he was getting from Xtele.

"Hey, Rich, can we go back for a minute?" Jen asked after Rich had finished. "How are you coaching—"

"Our competitors are giving big discounts," Rich went on, cutting Jen off completely, "and I think that's where we're getting killed right now."

There was an uncomfortable silence in the grand room for a few moments. Jen and Michelle exchanged knowing glances. Allan shifted uneasily in his chair. Everyone was on edge awaiting Mark's response.

"We're not known as the cheapest provider." Mark pursed his lips. "We're the quality play. That's one thing that differentiates us. We're not sacrificing margins."

"I know," Rich argued, "but it's hard to compete when Xtele is selling so cheap, and everyone else is discounting twenty percent on already lower prices. We've got to stay competitive."

"Damn it, Rich—you know Gold will never go for discounts! We may as well pack up our stuff now if that's all we've got." Mark slammed the table with both hands.

Michelle stood up as she presented several operational improvements she was in the process of implementing, explaining how they would improve efficiency by twenty-five percent.

"We need to be completely sure of those numbers." Mark looked at Michelle and then Allan. "If we're off, the board's going to be up our ass!"

"Agreed." Michelle started to walk laps around the long boardroom table at a head-turning pace.

"Really, Michelle?" Allan's eyes got wide. "You're like the Energizer Bunny!"

"You know I can't sit still!" Michelle exclaimed. "We ops folks gotta walk the floor."

"If you say so." Allan shook his head and shifted his focus back to the group. "Look, everyone, Michelle and I are scheduled to go through the numbers again to explore more opportunities later today."

Everyone in the room seemed energized and ready to execute their action plans. Mark adjusted the collar of his light gray dress shirt and smiled slightly. He turned to his head of HR.

"Okay, Jen, you're up."

Jen passed her presentation handouts to everyone in the room. The team rustled through the pages.

Jen cleared her throat. "The good news is that our time to fill open positions is down, so we're hiring faster. As you can see, turnover is steady. We've reached out to ten more candidates for the R&D director role this quarter, so we're still pounding the pavement on that search. We've held down our HR operating costs from last year's cut, and our employee claims and injuries are also down. All in all, I'd say we're headed in the right direction . . ."

Sensing a subtle change in the room's energy, Jen paused and glanced up from her handout. Everyone had their faces buried in her printouts, and she couldn't read their expressions as usual.

"Okay, let's continue with an update on benefits: We're finishing open enrollment prep. More good news—our benefit carriers are only raising prices two percent compared to the standard five percent. Allan and I thought it'd be a great idea to split the two percent between the employees and Dominal to show we're all in this together while also helping profitability." Jen glanced at Allan.

Mark looked at Allan to gauge his response. Allan gave a small nod to Jen and then focused back on his handouts, apparently avoiding Mark's gaze.

"Finally, on the last slide"—Jen flipped the page—"I'd like to talk about our cultural initiatives. We have a company-wide survey launching next month, which should help give us some insight into turnover."

"Thank you, Jen." Mark glanced around the room. "Anyone have any questions or feedback?"

No one made eye contact with Mark or Jen. The lack of interest was palpable. Jen felt defeated and wondered why the leadership team was showing such apathy for a key area like HR.

"Way to push the paper forward," Rich said sarcastically while turning his head to Jen. "As usual, we're all on the edge of our seats with the HR update."

"Knock it off, Rich," Mark snapped. "If you have constructive feedback, be professional and share it."

"Nothing to add." Rich sulked. "Sorry."

"Okay, thanks everyone." Mark wrapped up the meeting. "We're getting there, but there's still a ton of work to do. Let's meet again tomorrow."

"Thanks for making the time to meet with me, Mark."

"My pleasure, Meg. Give me one second." The intense, late afternoon sun was causing a glare on his Zoom call, so he adjusted his screen to see Meg clearly.

"No problem." Meg sat in her home office with the unusual, gentle pitter-patter of Los Angeles rain hitting the windows. "It's nice to be face-to-face, albeit over video. Were my initial comments on Jen's deck helpful?"

"Yes, very much so. Appreciate you sending those over."

"Sure. What else can I do to help?"

"Well . . ." Mark wrung his hands. "Like I said in my email, we're in the fight of our life. We just did a first review of board presentations, and the sales, ops, and finance plans are making progress, but I'm worried we're going to get creamed on HR."

"I've worked with companies backed by Gold in the past," Meg said slowly. "They're intense. You're really going to have to be crisp and buttoned-up."

"Yeah, exactly!" Mark's eyes were wide. "But you saw Jen's slides. You know the board couldn't care less about any of that right now. We're bleeding people!"

"You need specific actions."

"Yes, we need actions!" Mark sat back in his chair. "Real, hard-hitting actions! Not crap and spin and future surveys! Ugh, sorry, Meg, I don't mean to lose my cool."

"No worries, I get it." Meg smoothed her favorite black-and-white sweater with a hint of silver thread. She always felt these

small embellishments brought her personality into a professional setting without being over the top. "Did you give Jen
feedback?"

"I didn't." Mark glanced out the window. "And yes, I know
I need to . . . she deserves at least that. But I'm struggling with
what to tell her. Jesus, I'm doing a crappy job leading her."

"Hey, go easy on yourself." Meg tucked her short, blonde
hair behind her ears. "What you are going through is tough,
really tough. And even in normal circumstances, no CEO can
solve every problem for every person on his leadership team.
Part of being a good leader is acknowledging when someone
needs support that you can't provide."

"Yeah, to be honest, Meg . . ." Mark cast his eyes toward the
ceiling. "I feel like I've let the team down. I'm usually so good
at spotting trends. Hell, it led to the end of my career at Davis &
Edwards because I was so adamant about what I believed would
happen. How did I miss Xtele?"

"No one can predict every trend." Meg noticed a large pud-
dle forming outside the French door of her office. She looked
back at Mark. "How long have you been CEO?"

"About eighteen months." Mark rubbed his eyes. "Took over
from the founder when we sold to Gold."

"Is this your first CEO job?"

"Yeah, before this, I was the chief strategy officer at Davis
& Edwards for years. I saw the market fundamentally shifting
and couldn't get anyone to agree that we needed to change our
business model. They ended up asking me to leave."

"I've heard the story," Meg acknowledged. "I'm sure that was hard. Especially because you were right in the end."

"Yeah, I knew the challenges would be different as CEO, so I've really been focused on building the team." Mark looked away from the screen and put his head in his hands. "You know, maybe I just took my eye off the ball."

"Or maybe this wasn't something you could have seen coming." Meg tried to make eye contact with Mark. "Look, there's no point in dwelling on the past—you're focused now on mitigating this threat, right?"

"Yeah, but I am still struggling with Jen." Mark shook his head. "You know, I really strive to be a servant leader, but . . . right now, I feel like I just don't have it in me. I need her to step up."

"Okay, Mark—first, we're having this conversation on the best way to help her, so that's exactly how you're guiding her," Meg said. "And second, you have to figure out the best use of your time. Dwelling on this situation with Jen is only using up your energy when you should be focused on getting ready for this meeting with Gold."

"You're right." Mark sat up in his chair. "Listen, do you have time to help Jen get this presentation ready?"

"I will make time. But it's up to you to talk to Jen about it. I can't force her to accept my help."

"Yeah." Mark adjusted his glasses. "Any thoughts on how I should approach it?"

"Well, maybe start from a place of curiosity. Ask her what she thought the board's reaction would be to what she presented."

Mark shook his head. "She'll most likely respond with, 'As usual, no engagement.' They never have anything to say."

"That's a problem, right? Given the issues you've highlighted." Meg took a sip of water. "I mean, you need the board to engage with what she presents."

"I do." Mark tapped his pen on the desk. "The problem is I don't think she's ever thought about it that way."

"Yeah, you're probably right," Meg agreed. "Her presentation is a tactical department summary when you need it to be a company growth action plan. Perhaps you can help her understand that leaders at this level are focused on the latter."

"That's good." Mark jotted down notes. "I may use that with all of my team."

"Look, the key to your approach is to be curious, not furious. Listen to what she has to say, and address it in a way that feels natural to you. You will guide her to the right answer."

"Ha!" Mark chuckled. "I love the 'be curious, not furious.' That's great. I'll give it a try."

⋆

After lunch, Mark trudged down the hallway to Jen's office. He paused to look at his favorite award: Fastest Growing Company 2016. They'd earned it the year he'd joined the company. He smiled, remembering the excitement he and George had felt when they'd won and the fancy ceremony he and Leanne had attended to receive the award on behalf of Dominal.

Mark sighed and continued down the hall, reflecting on his conversation with Meg and trying to prepare himself for the discussion he was about to have with Jen.

Just outside her office, he stopped, looked down at his black dress shoes, inhaled, and held it. After slowly releasing his breath, he walked through the door. "Have a few minutes, Jen?"

"Yeah, hey, sure. Have a seat." Jen cleared the empty lunch containers from her desk and threw them in the trash. "What can I do for you?"

Mark sat down and glanced around Jen's office. Her tattered particle board desk was on its last legs and had probably been around since Dominal was founded. Clearly, she had tried to brighten the space with some colorful abstract art pieces that matched the hideous pieces in his office, but they felt out of place. On her credenza, Mark noticed the single picture of her family posing by the 2016 Cubs World Series Trophy. He made a mental note that she deserved better furniture once Dominal got itself out of its current predicament.

"So, I wanted to talk to you about your board presentation."

"Sure." Jen pulled out a pad of paper from a drawer in the rickety desk. "What's up?"

"Well, let me ask you, what did you think the board's reaction would be to what you presented today?"

"Umm . . ." Jen seemed to stall for time. "Well, I don't really know. For the most part, it's the usual presentation we give to the board, but I modified it to focus on how we were going to address the turnover issue and to provide more detail on the R&D search like you asked."

"And given the pressure we're under, how did you think they'd respond?"

"Sorry." Jen had a puzzled look. "I don't follow."

"Okay." Mark brushed a speck off his gray slacks. "Did you think they'd feel like we have it under control and can fix the problems based on what you presented?"

"Well, I guess. I thought that's what I covered in my slides." Jen sighed. "I mean, it's not like they really have a lot to say about HR."

"But don't they?" Mark argued. "I mean, they're all over us about turnover and open positions. Isn't that HR?"

"Yeah, I guess." Jen looked down. "But they never seem to want to talk about what I present."

"True." Mark angled his head to the side. "And part of that's my fault. I should've provided you with more guidance on how to engage them. So, let me try to start with that now. Look, what you presented today is a great tactical HR summary, but it's not a board presentation."

Jen shook her head. "I don't follow."

"There weren't enough tangible actions in your plan and too many check-the-box activities that aren't going to help us get out of our current situation. We need more hard-hitting actions from HR."

"Okay," Jen's eyes widened. "But this is what HR does. I want to help, but you have to give me more direction. I'm not a mind reader."

"Yes, and I'm not an HR person, and neither are our board members." Mark put a hand on each of the chair's armrests. "So, you need to think about this more as a company-level action plan. What are you going to do that is going to help Dominal solve its business problems? This is *your* area. You've got to figure out the right action steps, just like me and everyone else on the leadership team."

Jen looked down at her hands in her lap. Mark could sense her frustration.

"I know you and Shauna have been working hard on this, but this just isn't working. We need a new approach." Mark tried to get back to Meg's guidance—to be curious, not furious. "How did your meeting go with Meg Beecham?"

"We met last week when she was in town." Jen looked up. "She is clearly smart. I plan to work with her as I have time. She's just a bit . . . you know . . . different. Her first assignment was for me to watch *The Karate Kid* again. Anyway, Dave and I watched it—but I have no idea why. And now Dave's practicing all the karate moves he picked up, and it's driving me nuts!" Jen forced a thin smile.

Mark chuckled. "I remember that movie well. Ralph Macchio. Mr. Miyagi, right?" Jen nodded, and Mark was quiet for a few moments.

"Look, Jen," he said gently. "I took the liberty of reaching out to Meg to discuss your presentation today. I think the two of you should go through it as soon as possible. She had some good initial thoughts based on our short conversation."

Jen's head shot back. "Well, I was planning to work with her."

"Yeah, I know. Don't take it personally, I wasn't trying to go behind your back. I know I can't give you the guidance you need to solve this problem, but I can give you a resource. Meg is someone who can help you right now. We need her. You need her."

Jen's shoulders slumped. "Okay."

"Reach out to her and get on the phone with her first thing tomorrow. We need new ideas ASAP."

9 781647 049409